AFTER THE FLOOD

Recent Titles by Peter Turnbull

AND DID MURDER HIM
CONDITION PURPLE
DEATHTRAP*
KILLING FLOOR
LONG DAY MONDAY
THE MAN WITH NO FACE
PERILS AND DANGERS*
THE RETURN*
TWO WAY CUT

* *available from Severn House*

AFTER THE FLOOD

Peter Turnbull

This first world edition published in Great Britain 2002 by
SEVERN HOUSE PUBLISHERS LTD of
9–15 High Street, Sutton, Surrey SM1 1DF.
This first world edition published in the USA 2002 by
SEVERN HOUSE PUBLISHERS INC of
595 Madison Avenue, New York, N.Y. 10022.

British Library Cataloguing in Publication Data

Turnbull, Peter, 1950–
   After the flood
   1. Hennessey, Chief Inspector (Fictitious character) – Fiction
   2. Yellich, Sergeant (Fictitious character) – Fiction
   3. Police – England – Yorkshire – Fiction
   4. Detective and mystery stories
   I. Title
   823.9'14 [F]

ISBN 0-7278-5745-2

Typeset by Palimpsest Book Production Ltd.,
Polmont, Stirlingshire, Scotland.
Printed and bound in Great Britain by
MPG Books Ltd., Bodmin, Cornwall.

One

. . . After the flood

THURSDAY 31 MARCH

The flood came in late March. It remained for just three days but in those three days the citizens of York were once again reminded of the drawback of living in the beautiful, ancient city. At its height, the flood waters were two feet deep above pavement level; the terraced houses that were close to the River Ouse were, as usual, badly affected, cellars flooded completely and everything therein ruined. The householders had to carry what they could to upstairs rooms and just wait for the waters to recede, after which, with good humour if possible, they brushed the remaining water from their living rooms, pumped out their cellars, jettisoned carpets and other possessions that had been ruined and then wrote for an insurance claim form. The city of York will flood once every two or three years, to greater or lesser levels of seriousness, and sometimes with the occasional fatality, as with a man comatose because of alcohol excess lying in an alley, or the down-and-out sleeping in a shed on an allotment. Equally tragically, for humans often bond with animals more than they do with other humans, there will be the loss of pets that could not escape the rising waters of the River Ouse. York will flood in the autumn because

1

falling leaves clog the drains and the rainfall cannot run off. But most often, if it floods it floods in the spring when the Ouse is swollen with rain and snow-melt from the upper reaches of Swaledale. After each flood, the first thing that any property owner does – whether the occupier of a small terraced house or a large farm – is to walk his or her property to assess the extent of the damage.

John Brand walked his farm. Eight hundred acres of arable, but the meadows which banked on to the Ouse he gave over to pasture, for he bred Gloucester Old Spots as an indulgence, as a contribution to keeping, if not a rare then at least an obscure breed of pig from extinction, rather than as a commercial venture. Though he did have an arrangement with a maker of 'real sausages' in York, who would buy a pig for slaughter and with its sweet meat produce pork-and-beer sausages, which sold well. Very well indeed. Brand's arable land had escaped the flooding and, having taken his stock to higher ground when the rain showed no sign of letting up, he walked the pasture really more as a psychological exercise, a man reclaiming his land from the river. With his a flat cap, wax jacket over a green military-style pullover, corduroy trousers and wellington boots, and two border collies at his feet, an observer would see him as the very image of a countryman. The landscape about him was flat, desolate, brown and green, sodden; pools of water stood trapped in the fields and the sky was grey and overcast.

John Brand walked to the river's edge and stood on the bank looking down at the smooth but powerfully flowing Ouse. Brand knew she was not a river to mess with; she had claimed her lives over the years. He turned to his right, walking northwards with the low townscape and the square tower of the Minster behind him on the southern skyline, and walked the edge of the river, lamenting the carcass of a black-faced ewe which had clearly been caught up in the Dales and had fetched up here on the river's edge just to the north of York. Brand took solid canvas working gloves from his pocket, put them on, knelt down, took hold of the rear leg of the sheep and pulled it further up the bank to where it was unlikely to be reclaimed by the river. The 'townies' and the tourists, he reasoned, were sensitive souls and would not care to see the carcass of a sheep floating by. The sheep might still be fresh enough to be of interest to a fox; if not, the rats and other creatures of the riverbanks would begin the process of decomposition, and when it had dried out a little, and the weather become warmer, the flies would arrive and complete the process. He took the gloves off, put them back in the pocket of his wax jacket and walked on towards the beck. The beck flowed from a distant source but cut across his land and joined the river at an angle of ninety degrees. It cut a deep trough, about four feet wide and in places equally deep. At that moment it was as he expected, in a state of spate, as the last of the flood drained into the river. The beck was too fast-flowing, too wide and deep, to permit him to jump across and continue his walk along the bank and so he turned and followed the curve of the beck inland, away from the river, towards his fields of arable.

Then one, and then the other, of his dogs pointed. Every dog points, but each in a different way and not all as clearly as the classic raised paw and straight tail of the 'pointers'. Brand long ago recognised the point of his dogs: standing rigidly still, heads cocked to one side, eyes fixed on the object of interest. He followed their point, and saw it too – an arm, human, bones, a skeleton. He approached it cautiously; his dogs followed reluctantly. The skeleton was wedged half in and half out of the bank of the beck, one arm rising and falling in a grotesque waving motion with the movement of the rushing water, the skull grinning at him.

He stepped back, turned and hurried to his house. Not one for mobile phones, he had to use a landline to call the police. He hurried because, although the person was long dead, he believed the working of the beck would dislodge the skeleton. The beck had already exposed it; it would eventually be dislodged, taken into the river and lost.

Louise D'Acre took the call at 10.30 a.m. She sat in her office next to the pathology laboratory at the York City Hospital, reading a report she had put in for typing the previous day and which had been returned for checking. She had notoriously bad handwriting which the clerical staff at the hospital had slowly learned to decipher but which often still resulted in the occasional howler. This particular report was a post-mortem of the suicide of a young man whose personality tended to deep depressions and the report had been returned to her speaking of a 'black whore' of depression in respect of the state of mind of the young man when he took his own life. As powerful as the image might be, and amusing in its mistake, it had to go. D'Acre took her pen, crossed out 'whore' and wrote *wave* above the word.

It was then that her telephone rang. She picked up the receiver, answered it, and at the same time reached for her notepad and listened as she scribbled down directions in a hand only she could read. She replaced the phone and wound herself into a trench coat which was too large for her but with a tightened belt looked very fetching, placed a waterproof hat on her head, picked up her black bag and left her office. She walked out of the slab-sided medium-rise hospital to the car park and drove out of the city to the north, following the directions she had been given. She reached the village of Coddington and parked her car in the high street, placing a DOCTOR ON CALL sign in the windscreen.

The village seemed to be linear, built on either side of a long street, and the houses didn't seem to extend back very far beyond the main road. There was a post office, a pub with a wagon wheel mounted high on the wall, a shop, another shop, another pub . . . The road was wet and muddy, and the tidemarks on the buildings spoke of the recent flood. The whole mood of the village, it seemed to her, was tired after exertion, effete, in a word. It was still and, save for the cawing of rooks, quite silent. It was, she thought, like a boxing ring where a title fight had just taken place, where there was emptiness but still an 'atmosphere', where you could still smell the sweat. Except in Coddington that Friday morning it wasn't sweat which teased her nostrils, it was the smell left by swollen and burst drains. Just one other figure was in the main street, a young constable. He stood a few hundred yards from where she had parked her car, raised a hand and began to walk towards her. Louise D'Acre picked up her bag from the rear seat of the car, locked the vehicle and walked towards the officer.

'Dr D'Acre?' The constable asked deferentially when within speaking distance.

'For my sins, 'tis me,' Louise D'Acre said.

'I've been asked to escort you to the scene, ma'am. Chief Inspector Hennessey told me what car to look for – distinctive, he said.'

'Very.' D'Acre and the constable began to walk side by side. 'This is the first time it's been out for a few days . . . I rent a car during the floods.'

'Sensible, ma'am: she looks too valuable to risk losing.'

'More sentimental value to me. It was my father's first and only car, though, having said that, I have had some very interesting offers for her.'

'Really? Sorry, ma'am, may I carry your bag?'

'Thank you.' D'Acre handed her black bag to the officer. They continued to walk side by side, the constable perhaps half a step behind D'Acre and on the outside of her, and in silence until the officer said, 'Just down here, doctor.'

'Down here' proved to be a narrow pathway in which the gravel had been deeply cut by running water and which, D'Acre could see, led to muddy green-brown fields, a flurry of police activity, a white Land-Rover and a blue and white police tape encircling something on the ground. D'Acre stepped over a wooden stile into the field and regretted not bringing stronger shoes. Her shoes were not dainty, but she should have read the signs: the telephone message had told her of 'apparent human remains in a field'; she knew what the weather had been like for the last few days. She also regretted not changing into green coveralls at the hospital; she felt the flimsiness of her clothes and yearned for riding boots, jodhpurs and a warm jacket. But she pressed on and was met by a smiling Chief Inspector Hennessey who, she noticed, had tucked his trouser-bottoms into his socks.

'You missed the fun,' he said.

'Oh, really?' D'Acre returned the smile but permitted only the briefest eye contact.

'Spent the morning building mud pies, didn't we, constable?'

'Yes, sir,' the constable replied sheepishly.

'Mud pies?' D'Acre took her bag from the constable.

'Well, diverted a stream – plenty of manpower and a small earthmover that was requisitioned. It was in the village anyway, digging out silted-up ditches. The fella was only too pleased to help.'

'Help?'

'Diverting the stream. This way, I'll show you.' Hennessey led the forensic pathologist across the field, holding up the blue and white tape for her to lower herself under, and towards the mound covered by a sheet of heavy-duty plastic.

Closer at hand Louise D'Acre saw that the sheet of plastic was draped over the side of the path of a stream, now without running water but still very muddy. She glanced up the stream and saw that a dam had been built and that the stream, as Hennessey had said, had indeed been diverted across a neighbouring field and into the Ouse. She turned to him. 'Bet you thought you'd dammed up your last stream?'

'Indeed I did. More years ago than I care to remember.' Then a pained look crossed his eyes and Louise D'Acre didn't pursue the conversation. 'So, what have we?'

'Constable.' Hennessey addressed a second, older constable, who bent down and lifted the plastic sheeting.

'Female.' Dr D'Acre looked at the remains. 'Definitely a she . . . completely skeletal, so she must have been buried for a good number of years. These wet clays will preserve flesh quite well. Strange place to bury a body, so close to a stream.'

'The farmer . . .' Hennessey nodded to the constable, who let the plastic sheet fall back into place, 'he found the body. He told me that the stream "wanders", as he put it. Noticeably so, over a period of years.'

'Yes . . . I have heard that watercourses do that. You know, in Ireland, they can't pinpoint the actual site of the Battle of the Boyne like we can pinpoint Naseby or Marston Moor, because the Boyne has altered its course so much in the last four hundred years. So she probably wasn't buried so near the stream after all, but time and flood . . . Well, I can't do anything here. I can do the p.m. this afternoon. It's been quiet in the Vale, no recent murders whose post-mortems have to take priority. She could have been down there for several hundred years, of course. I didn't see any clothing or modern knick-knacks like watches.'

'That would be a pleasantly neat end to the working week. I have this weekend off.'

'More than seventy years in the clay and you lose interest, I gather?'

'That's the cut-off point.' A sudden gust of wind tugged at Chief Inspector Hennessey's silver hair. 'Little point in opening an inquiry when the perpetrator is going to be in his late eighties at the very least. More pressing crimes to solve with limited resources.'

'Indeed.' Louise D'Acre looked at the skeleton, the top side of the skull protruding from the wet soil, the lower left arm also protruding, as was the left pelvic bone. 'She – and it's definitely female, as I said – she's still more concealed than revealed. I'll have to supervise the removal . . . a careful peeling-away of the surrounding soil, and sifting of the same, for your ends, not mine.'

Hennessey glanced at her questioningly.

'Well, you could shovel away the murder weapon and not know it.'

'Of course . . .' Hennessey felt a surge of embarrassment. 'Of course . . . right, sergeant!'

'Sir?'

'Two constables with spades, please.'

'Sir!' The sergeant turned and called to a group of officers. 'Constable Cheapside, Constable Neilson . . .

shovels . . . Take your directions from the pathologist . . . Come on, sharply now!'

Louise D'Acre stood close by the side of the route of the original stream, which was by now a trench, though not so close as to intimidate the two constables, who dug gently, one spit of a spade at a time, into the sodden clay. One constable slowly, carefully excavated the skull, and the other, at D'Acre's suggestion, worked downwards from the pelvic bone towards the foot, so as not to get in each other's way. Both constables placed the clay they removed into a sieve, which, when full, was removed by a third constable and replaced with an empty sieve. George Hennessey stood further back from the crime scene, close enough to show interest but far enough away to enjoy the luxury of being able to look around him: the flatness of this part of England, the huge sky it afforded, distant church spires, a skein of geese flying north, two magpies hopping about the hedgerow. A traditionally rare bird, Hennessey had noted, and had read in the press that the numbers of the species had grown in recent years, but would, the newspaper article promised, subside to normal numbers in time.

'Oh!'

The sudden cry from one of the constables brought Hennessey's attention back to the matter in hand. He saw the constable who had been asked to dig around the skull leap backwards. Louise D'Acre stepped forwards. 'Don't touch it,' she said, softly but authoritatively. She turned to Hennessey. 'We'll need a stretcher now, please.'

'Sergeant. Stretcher.'

'Sir!'

Hennessey strode forwards as D'Acre grittily, he thought, no longer worried about getting her city clothing muddy, clambered into the stream bed, knelt and picked up the skull. She turned it over in her hands, examining the base and the cranium.

'Whoever did this was making sure all right.' She raised her voice for Hennessey to hear her but didn't look at him, continuing to focus on the skull. 'The head was severed from the rest of the body. Somebody was making sure she was dead.'

'Murder?'

D'Acre now turned to Hennessey and smiled. 'Don't be in a rush to be the policeman. Medieval beliefs in witchcraft and sorcery often drove folk to chop off the heads of people whose condition defied current medical knowledge. Not usually in England, though, but it wasn't unknown. The Dracula legend and the concept of "undead" comes from eastern Europe, as does the practice of driving a stake through the heart of those who weren't awake but refused to decompose. The "undead" concerned would be in a coma or a persistent vegetative state, but to superstitious people such a condition could only be the work of the devil. We don't know how old this skeleton is . . . it could be centuries old.' She continued to examine the skull. 'There's nothing . . . Hello!'

'Found something?'

'Yes.' She brushed away a thin film of clay and then Hennessey saw it too, glinting in the modest amount of daylight that prevailed.

'A filling. A gold filling.'

'Well, that's not medieval,' he sighed.

'It isn't, is it? But gold won't rust, so it still could be the victim of a murder that occurred more than seventy years ago. I can't . . . I won't say any more until the post-mortem.'

'Understood.'

Dr D'Acre clambered out of the ditch and placed the

skull in a productions bag, sealed it and placed the bag on the stretcher, which had been placed close to where the constables had been digging.

'Frighten you?' Hennessey heard D'Acre ask, smiling, of the constable whose spade had dislodged the skull. He liked her for that.

'A little, ma'am, yes.'

'Means you're human. How long have you been a police officer?'

'Less than a year, ma'am.'

'Thought I hadn't met you before, Constable . . . ?'

'Cheapside, ma'am.'

'Well, what happened to you just then, Constable Cheapside, is nothing compared to what you will experience. Ever scraped the victims of a road traffic accident off the road?'

'No . . . not yet, ma'am.'

'You will . . . When you've done that a time or two, you'll take skeletal remains in your stride.'

'Ma'am.'

'Now, use your spade and work down from where the skull was. You'll come to the shoulder blades and ribcage.'

'Ma'am.'

A camera flashed as the scene-of-crimes officer photographed the procedure. The man didn't need to be told what to photograph; his brief, as always, was simple: photograph everything from every angle, in colour and in black and white.

Constables Cheapside and Neilson continued to chip delicately away by the skeleton, placing the muddy soil in the sieves, which were taken to the route of the diverted stream, where the mud was sifted for any artefacts. Presently, after ninety minutes' careful, painstaking work, the skeleton lay fully exposed in the side of the original course of the stream. The SOCO stepped forward and took more photographs, again from all angles.

'One adult female.' Louise D'Acre glanced down at the headless skeleton. 'I can't see any sign of trauma to the corpse and there was none to the head.' She turned to Hennessey. 'I think somebody was just making sure, as I said.'

'You think?'

'Well . . .' Louise D'Acre took her foot from a puddle and placed it in an area of softer mud, which proceeded to fill up with water, again covering her shoe. 'Oh . . . should have changed. Nobody to blame but myself . . . What was I saying?'

Hennessey reminded her. 'Making sure.'

'Oh yes, in the nineteenth century, particularly during epidemics, cholera, typhoid and so on, there were many premature proclamations of death. Stories abound of people wriggling to the surface of a pile of bodies in a cholera pit, or church wardens hearing the cries for help from beneath the ground in a churchyard . . .'

'Hardly bears thinking about.'

'But it happened, and the medical profession were forced to concede that only two symptoms meant that a corpse was dead beyond question: the onset of putrefaction and severance of head from body.' Hennessey, widely read though not educated, wondered where else a head could be severed from. 'Either of these two symptoms and you have death. So if the victim here was strangled, for example, then chopping off the head would be a means of making sure that she was indeed deceased. But I think I've done all I can here. If you could convey the deceased back to York City, I'll do the p.m. this afternoon. I'll go home and change now.' Dr D'Acre smiled and raised her eyebrows. 'One unexpected dry-cleaning bill to pay.' She glanced at her coat, which was caked with mud near the hem, then opened it. 'My skirt didn't escape either. Will you be representing the police at the post-mortem, inspector?'

'Yes . . . yes, I will.'

'Shall we say 2 p.m.?'

'I'll be there.'

'Well . . .' Louise D'Acre, dressed in a green lightweight coverall smock, mouth-gauze, latex gloves and disposable headwear, adjusted the stainless-steel anglepoise arm above the dissecting table, at the end of which was a microphone. The room was brightly illuminated by filament bulbs contained behind frosted perspex sheets. 'The deceased is skeletal . . . appears to be an adult female.' She picked up the finger bones of the hand of the skeleton and said, 'The bones are human,' then turned to Hennessey and explained, 'A formality, but it has to be observed.'

'Of course.'

'The anatomical skeletons made out of resin used by medical students and inevitably christened "Humphrey" or "Gertrude" have turned up in the wrong places and caused consternation. But resin is significantly lighter in weight than human bone and I would have recognised a resin skeleton at the scene.'

'Of course.'

'In North America the skeletal remains of a bear's paw have been mistaken for human bones . . . but this is human. So, we are in business.' She then spoke clearly for the benefit of the microphone and the audio typist who would, later that day or the next, be typing up her verbal report. 'The deceased was an adult female at the time of her death. Immediately obvious is that the skull has been severed at the first vertebra, but left in the same location as the remainder of the body. Skeletalisation is complete; there are no remnants of putrefaction . . . no possible identifying artefacts such as rings or other jewellery . . . no indication of clothing.' Dr D'Acre stepped back from the table and turned to Hennessey. 'She was buried naked.'

'She was?'

'Yes . . . and any jewellery or watch was removed. You didn't find any metal or other non-biodegradable item in the mud taken from around the skeleton?'

'We didn't.'

'Well, all of us wear something that is non-biodegradable. All clothing has metal – hooks, zip fasteners – and it also often has non-biodegradable parts – plastic buttons, toggles from duffel coats . . . Then we all wear metal as decoration or for function: brooches, rings, wristwatches.'

'Yes, but nothing of the sort was found?'

'All removed, most likely to hinder identification.'

'Most likely.'

'But they left us the head, with all those lovely teeth to match against dental records. Especially after going to the length of chopping the head off . . . if he – or she, or they – had buried the head separately, or just chucked it into the river, so easy from where the skeleton was buried, if that had been done, we would be most unlikely to have identified her.'

'Lucky for us, then?'

'I'll say.'

'And for her family too, they'll be grieving.'

'She has a family?'

'She gave birth, and did so more than once – but we'll

14

come on to that.' Louise D'Acre then spoke once again for the benefit of the microphone. 'There are no other signs of trauma to the body. And because the body was deeply buried, putrefaction would have come from primary invaders: bacterial flora in the gastrointestinal tract which invade the vascular system and eventually spread throughout the body.'

This last was clearly for the benefit of Hennessey, who said, 'I see.'

'As opposed to secondary invaders, ye olde *Musca domestica*, for instance.'

'The what?'

'Ye common housefly, chief inspector. Size for size it puts vultures to shame. It has the ability to scent rotting flesh from up to four miles away in calm, warm conditions, but only invades to lay its maggots if the flesh is exposed. So primary invaders did the work here.'

She paused. 'Now, examining the severance of the head . . . there are striations in the base, an indication that the severance was done by means of sawing. The sawing was done neatly between the vertebrae . . . between C1 and C2, striations noted on C2 as well as on C1. By observation of the skull and the pelvis, and the smaller, finer femur, the skeleton is that of a woman. But what determines the sex of this person in life is the pubic scarring which is observed.' She turned to Hennessey. 'During childbirth, scarring of the pubic bones occurs when the tendon insertions and periosteum are torn. She was a she, and she had had at least two children, possibly more.'

'Noted,' Hennessey said. 'That will help us identify her.'

'Now, two more questions remain to be answered. Age at death should be no problem – we'll extract a tooth and cut it into a cross-section, and that will give us the age at the time she died, plus or minus twelve months. When she was buried . . . well, more than ten years ago.'

'You can tell that?'

'Well, all the periosteum that I mentioned earlier is absent. Periosteum is a membrane which covers areas of bone not covered by cartilage. Cartilage and ligaments decay and disappear after about twelve months, but periosteum is very hardy, very durable, and will last for ten years before decaying completely. So ten years is minimum, could be more than ten years she's been in the clay, fifteen, twenty even.'

'I see. All good information.'

'Just earning my crust, chief inspector,' Dr D'Acre said with a smile which could be 'heard' behind her facemask. 'Can we have a photograph of this striation, please?' She turned to the rotund man who Hennessey always found to be jovial and warm-hearted, despite his job.

Eric Filey, also dressed in disinfected, lightweight green coveralls, advance to the skeleton, focused the lens of the camera and took a series of rapid close-up stills of the damage done to the vertebrae by the blade of the saw. That done, he retired to the far side of the instrument trolley.

Dr D'Acre took a long, thin stainless-steel rod from the instrument trolley, gently inserted it into the mouth and prised the jaws open. They fell apart silently. 'Might have been some resistance,' she explained to Hennessey. 'No rigor because there's no flesh, but the mandible bones might have fused with time.'

'Ah . . .' Hennessey's eyes were still recovering from the flash of Eric Filey's camera.

'So . . . Well, the deceased was a lady who knew the value of dental hygiene and, although I am no odontologist, I would identify the work as being British dentistry. She has lost one incisor from the upper teeth – she probably wore a denture – but the majority of the dental work has been done on the lower teeth. There should be dental records somewhere, with luck.'

'With luck,' Hennessey echoed. 'It's often all about luck, hard relentless slog and luck.'

'So a female adult, white European – you can determine race from the skull and other parts of the skeleton, but the best identification of race comes from the teeth. Each racial type has its own distinct type of tooth. Mixed-race people can cause confusion, but I think it's safe to say she was a white European lady in life. Age at death, to be determined, but of middle years, the skull has fully knitted together. I'll extract a tooth from the upper set, leave the lower teeth intact to help identification with dental records. You know, the police need a national database of dental records of all missing people.'

'It would be nice . . . cost, as always, is the obstacle.'

'It would identify her in a flash.'

'Or a flicker of a screen.'

'As you say, but unfortunately you've got a lot of old-fashioned legwork to do. I can perhaps narrow down the time of disappearance – more than ten years ago because of the complete absence of periosteum – but the dental work . . . It's not primitive, late twentieth century, sticking my neck out . . . Don't go back more than twenty years, not at first. She was five feet . . .' D'Acre stretched a retractable metal tape measure along the length of the femur, 'about five feet six inches tall. That is an approximation. Or about 167 centimetres.'

'Of course.' Hennessey smiled. He knew better than to ask a forensic scientist to commit to any finding except the most obvious and irrefutable.

17

'I'll be able to get the result of the cross-section of the tooth to you by tomorrow morning, chief inspector.'

'Thank you.'

'So I think that about wraps it up. Cause of death uncertain, but nothing that involved trauma to the body, no head injuries for example, nobody knocked her teeth out. But plenty of other ways to skin a cat: strangulation, suffocation, poison . . . I'll check for poisoning, but the arsenic so beloved of our Victorian forefathers is very uncommon these days. You can't just go into a chemist shop and buy it like they used to do. Lucky for us, I say.'

'Indeed.'

'Date of death? Well, ten to twenty years ago . . . but a person who would have been missed. She kept her dental appointments, so she valued herself, and so would be socially integrated, amongst her neighbours if nobody else, but more so because she gave birth, and more than once. So some now-adult children will be still wondering what happened to their mum.'

'That's plenty for us to go on. Thanks, Dr D'Acre.'

'I'll fax my report to you as soon as. And get the age at death to you as well.'

'Again, thanks.'

'So, if I don't see you again before the weekend, have a good one.'

'Thanks . . . it's my first full weekend for six weeks.'

'Doing anything with it?'

'No, nothing special.'

'Well, enjoy it anyway.'

George Hennessey disliked driving to the point of actually hating it, but he accepted it as a necessary part of early twenty-first century living, and after leaving York City

Hospital he took his car from the car park and returned to the crime scene. He drove up to the delightfully named Alice's Grange Farm, and knocked politely but firmly on the thickly varnished front door, setting dogs barking from within. The door was opened by a middle-aged lady in a pinafore with flour on her hands.

'Baking,' she explained, in an accent which was strong but not local.

'So I see. Sorry to bother you, madam.' Hennessey showed her his identity card. 'Is Mr Brand at home? It's him I want to see.'

'He's in the field. Dreadful business . . . a skeleton . . . I mean, I never. He's rediverting the beck to its original course. The police said he could.'

'Do you mind if I . . . ?'

'No, please . . . You'd be better going back on the road and picking up the footpath. The farmyard is a foot deep in the stuff.'

'Thanks. Appreciate the advice.'

'You can leave your car here, if you like.'

'I'll do that.' Hennessey glanced at the building. It seemed to him to be a traditional Vale of York farm building, squat, stone-built and with a solidly tiled roof, yet it had a certain newness about it.

'Bought it cheap and renovated it,' Brand explained when, a few minutes later, trouser-bottoms once again tucked into his socks, Hennessey stood in the field, being watched warily by Brand's border collies. In front of the two men the stream ran strongly, as if somehow happy to be on its original course, and had completely swallowed any trace of the excavation carried out a few hours earlier. 'Used to farm in Lincolnshire. Never could take to the county, but my wife comes from there.'

'Ah . . . I detected an accent that wasn't local. So that was a Lincolnshire accent?'

'From the Bourne area, born and bred.'

'One more to chalk up. When I came north all accents sounded the same, then I began to be able to tell the difference between Yorkshire and Lancashire.'

'That's not difficult.'

'It isn't now.' Hennessey smiled. 'Now I can tell Yorkshire-from-Sheffield, Yorkshire-from-Leeds, Yorkshire-from-York, Yorkshire-from-the-Dales, Yorkshire-from-the-coast.'

'You're a Londoner, by your accent?'

'Greenwich.'

'I'm from Norfolk originally. Our farm in Lincolnshire was flooded. It was quite unsettling: no indication of flooding, no heavy rain, all well at the close of the day, awoke the following morning and the whole area was like a swamp, but the river was back inside its banks . . . a bit creepy. I lost my crops. Other farmers lost livestock and two people were drowned. Didn't want to experience that again. So we came north, where it floods just the same.' Brand clearly enjoyed the joke against himself. 'We sold the farm in Lincolnshire and bought this one. We got it cheaply because it had been abandoned. Previous owner was elderly, let it run down, as elderly folk are wont to do with their property. So we got a good deal and set to work building it up again.'

'So how long have you lived here?'

'Eleven years this September.'

'And this field has always been pasture?'

'Of course.'

'Sorry, I don't farm.'

'Well, you won't get crops planted right next to a river, not unless there's a good dyke there. Can't plough up to a riverbank, can't take your crops on to high ground.'

'Of course.'

'So, yes, this has always been pasture. I keep my pigs here, Gloucester Old Spots, the orchard pig. They'll kill for apples, and produce the sweetest pork.'

'So if someone had been buried here you'd have noticed?'

'Oh, yes. Definitely.'

'So the body was buried before you came?'

'Yes, yes.' Brand pursed his lips. 'In fact, I'm no policeman or criminal, but an abandoned farm would be a good place to bury a body. The farm was derelict for four years before we bought it. The land was in a mess, the house was a ruin. The old boy, whose ghost my wife insists is still in the parlour, kept dogs, plenty of 'em. Had the run of the farm and by all accounts were not pet dogs, so we were told. And when they took his body away, the dogs had to be put down. So that gives you a time window of fourteen to eighteen years ago during which the body could have been buried, if it was buried when the farm was derelict.'

'It also suggests local knowledge.'

Two

In which one becomes two

George Hennessey arrived at Micklegate Bar Police Station at 8.30 a.m. He parked his car at the rear of the building, entered by the STAFF ONLY door, signed in and was sitting at his desk by 8.32. He picked up his telephone and punched in a four-figure internal number.

'Collator.' The response was quick, efficient.

'DCI Hennessey.'

'Yes, sir?'

'Anything for me?'

'Quite a bit, sir, came in overnight, as I thought it would.' The collator paused. 'Between ten and fifteen years ago, twenty women in their middle years were reported missing in the UK. In this area there were three. Shall I send the files up to you, sir?'

'Yes, please. We'll be getting information about the age at death later today I hope, but yes, if you could send them up I'll have a glance. You have selected by height as well?'

'About five feet six inches, yes, sir.'

'Good.' Hennessey replaced the phone gently. It rang again instantly. He snatched it up. 'Hennessey.'

'Dr D'Acre here.'

'Oh, yes?'

'The tooth . . . I extracted one of the upper molars from the skeleton we looked at yesterday and cut it in cross-section. It gave an age at death of fifty-three years, plus or minus twelve months.'

'Fifty-two to fifty-four years of age.' Hennessey scribbled on his notepad. 'Thank you very much. We have three ladies reported missing in the five-year time window we're looking at. The files are on the way up to me right now, and we'll see if any match. So, thanks again.'

One did. Her name was Amanda Dunney, fifty-three years of age when she was reported missing, twelve years ago. The photograph in the file showed a full-faced, flat-nosed woman, who wore her hair in a wide mop which just covered her ears. She was reported missing by her brother, Thomas Dunney of Whitby Road, Heworth. Hennessey stood and went down the CID corridor to Sergeant Yellich's office. He tapped on the door frame.

'Morning, skipper.' The fresh-faced younger man looked up and smiled at Hennessey.

'Got a job for you, Yellich. Doing anything pressing?'

'Writing up the burglary case. We nicked him yesterday afternoon.'

'So that's where you were.'

'Yes, skip. Good result. I mean seriously good. As often happens, the house was full of stolen goods and when we were there someone called to pick up the "stuff from the garage".' Yellich smiled. 'We were in plain clothes, you see. I mean very plain, because we had the house under surveillance, and we must have looked like crims, or the caller was assuming we were. He asked for the key to the garage, so Sid Bickerdyke said, "Help yourself, mate," so the fella reaches for the key from a row of keys. He knew which one it was all right. Went outside, went to the garage and came out with a parcel. Sid identified himself and the fella went as white as a sheet. Sid put the cuffs on him then clocked the parcel.'

'Cocaine?'

'Right lines, boss. Ecstasy tablets, one thousand of them. There's one rave that won't be very raving this weekend. Anyway, the fella's out of his depth, no previous, scared of jail and is plea-bargaining like his life depends on it, offering all sorts of information. We're breaking open a whole distribution network, and all from a phone call on Monday telling us to keep a watch on a garage.'

'Well, it sounds like you had more fun than I did. I was up to my ankles in mud in a field by the river.'

'The skeleton? I heard the boys talking about it.'

'The same. We have a possible ID here.' Hennessey held up the missing persons report. 'A lady, Amanda Dunney, went missing twelve years ago, right height, about five and a half feet, aged fifty-three years. I'd like you to go and talk to her brother, who reported her missing.

'Her brother? Wasn't she married then?'

'No. I picked that up too. It doesn't gel with what Dr D'Acre was able to tell us about the lady from her skeleton. But I won't tell you what. I'd like you to go and pick up the trail of Amanda Dunney, spinster of this parish, and find out all you can about her. We'll be releasing the story of the discovery of the skeleton to the press later today. I'd like her brother to be informed before he hears the news report.'

'Very good, boss.' Yellich stood. 'Assuming he's still alive.'

'As you say. His age is given here as fifty-six, so now he'll be sixty-eight . . . if he's still with us. We need to know who his sister's dentist was too.'

'I'll go and find what I find.' Yellich reached for his overcoat and hat. He glanced out of the window of his office; the ancient walls of the city glistened in the slight but incessant rainfall. The sky was low, grey, threatening. 'Fancy I'll need these.'

'Fancy you will. Her dentist, remember?'

'You're sure it's our Amanda?' Thomas Dunney gazed into the gas fire, which was turned down low, and didn't quite take the edge off the chill in the room. It was colder inside than was the air temperature outside: a house suffering badly from damp. Thomas Dunney was a frail, slightly built man, who wrapped himself in cardigans against the cold, three that Yellich could see, then a shirt, then a thermal vest. He wore corduroy trousers and his feet were encased in hiking boots and thick hiking socks. The room was cluttered – chairs and the settee seemed to have become receptacles for books, clothing and household items – and the carpet was sticky underfoot. Yellich could only imagine the state of the kitchen and bathroom. He was pleased he didn't have to search this house.

'We believe so, sir . . . We'll have to check the dental records, but the skeleton was aged at fifty-three years at the time of death, and my boss, who attended the crime scene, says the burial could be dated to the time that your sister disappeared.'

'Skeleton?'

'I'm afraid so. She was in the ground for a long time.'

There was a short silence, the Thomas Dunney said,

'That's her.' He nodded to the mantelpiece, to a photograph in an inexpensive frame. It showed a man and woman standing stiffly side by side. The man was short and slight, the woman was large. 'That's me and her.'

'I recognise you, sir. I assumed the lady to be your wife.'

'I never married. Neither did she. That was taken here, in the back garden. She disappeared a few years after that. She didn't like her photograph taken, she was self-conscious about her size. She was a big lady, she had to wear maternity smocks. She used to go shopping for them bang on nine o'clock in the morning, as soon as the shops opened, otherwise she'd be the only customer in the maternity-wear section who wasn't pregnant. We only really had each other.'

'Which dentist did she use?'

'Mr Serle. I use the same one. On Gillygate.'

Yellich scribbled the name on his pad.

'Do you know of anyone who would want to harm her?'

'Amanda? No. She was a nurse; no one would want to harm her.'

'I see. Where did she work? Which hospital?'

'She didn't. She was a practice nurse at a health centre; she also used to call on patients at their homes and administer medication, or she'd take blood and do blood-pressure checks in the health centre. She was that sort of nurse.'

'I read you gave her last address as Park Street, off The Mount.'

'Aye.'

Yellich continued to read the room. A print of the Madonna and child stood propped on the mantelpiece beside the photograph of Thomas and Amanda Dunney;

above the print, a set of rosary beads and a crucifix hung from a hook which had been screwed into the plaster. 'Was she a long time at that address?'

'Well, that was Amanda, she could never settle, always moving house, two years here, three years there. Always in York, though, where we were born and brought up.' The man sniffed and continued to gaze into the flames of the gas fire. 'We weren't that close really, me and her. She didn't approve of how I lived.' Thomas Dunney glanced round him. 'I like things like this. Amanda, she was fussy, neat, everything in its place, and she was one for cleanliness.'

'Nurses are like that. If they aren't when they join the profession, then they are at the conclusion of their training. So I believe.'

'Well, it was about this time of year, spring; I phoned her and her landlady said she hadn't seen her for a week. Got me worried . . . I mean we weren't close but she's still my sister. Phoned the health centre and they said she hadn't been at work for a fortnight. I went round to Park Street, her landlady told me again she hadn't seen her for a week, so I reported her missing. So now she's turned up – well, her skeleton has . . . foul play. Knew it, knew it . . . But Amanda had no enemies, a nurse doesn't. She hadn't much in the world. I took her clothes back here, kept them for six months, then gave them to a rag-and-bone man.'

'Any possessions?'

'Hardly any. A few books, a cassette/CD player, a few cassettes and CDs; not much to show for fifty-three years of life, thirty-five of which had been given to nursing. Who'd want to do that to our Amanda – kill her, then bury her body? Who, who'd want to do that? It's going to be an awful funeral, there'll be me and the priest and that's all. Dig her out of one hole and put her in another. But who'd want to do that to Amanda?'

'Plenty of folk would want to do that to "Big" Dunney. Plenty.'

'I take it she was not a friend of yours?'

'I rented a room to her – or did she rent it from me? I never know which is the correct way round. I rent rooms to professional ladies. Only women, no men; even gentlemen callers have to wait at the door, even in bad weather. The arrangement doesn't appeal to every woman; some take rooms in liberal-minded houses which actually allow men to stay overnight' – the woman shuddered – 'but equally, there are other women who appreciate the strict "no-men" regime. I dare say you could call us "bluestockings", although that phrase is a little out of fashion now.'

The woman was slender and white-haired, in a yellow dress and matching yellow shoes. She received Yellich in the front room of her house, which he found to be a complete contrast to Thomas Dunney's cramped and untidy home. This house was spacious, airy and neatly kept, smelling of furniture polish and air freshener. She was, thought Yellich, about sixty-five years of age.

'Miss Dunney had a room in the attic. The attic is divided widthways – that is, parallel with the line of the roof. Miss Dunney had the front room of those two rooms. She was here for about a year and a half.'

'She was a nurse, I understand?'

'She was. She was also "Amanda", until I found out a few things.'

'Oh?'

'She didn't tell me anything, but one day, about a month before she disappeared, she stopped going to work. She continued to leave the house as if going to work, but she was a woman who wore her emotions on her sleeve. She couldn't hide the fact that she was troubled. Never told me and I didn't ask. But a friend of mine is registered with a doctor at the health centre where Miss Dunney worked and told me that the nurse had been suspended. These things can't be hidden for ever, not in York. They may call it a city but it has the feel of a small town sometimes.'

'Do you know why she was suspended?'

'Yes, but it's not my place to tell you, young man, because all I can report is hearsay. But if you were to enquire at the health centre, get the information from the horse's mouth as it were, then you'll find out why plenty of people would like to murder her.'

'You've given her three names so far; which one was she known by?'

'All three . . .' The woman paused and listened as the front door opened, smiled and said, 'Good-morning, Mary.'

'Morning, Gwen,' Mary called from the hall. 'Just popped back for lunch.'

'I know all my residents. They all turn their keys in slightly different ways – some will fight the lock, others are more skilful, but all have their own way of unlocking the door. Where was I?'

'Three names you used for Amanda,' Yellich reminded her as Mary was heard stepping lightly up the stairs.

'All three. "Amanda" when she came, "Miss Dunney" when I heard the reason for her suspension, and the patients at the health centre began to refer to her as "Big Dunney" when the story emerged . . . and that was one of the mild names. I confess I was on the verge of asking her to leave when she disappeared. One day she didn't return at five thirty as she usually did, and eventually it was her brother that reported her missing . . . he could perhaps help you?'

'I've just come from his house.'

'Ah.'

'Which health centre did she work at?'

'Precentor's Court. In the city centre.'

'Did she have any friends?'

'Not that she would speak of. She did join a reading group that met every first Wednesday of the month.'

'A reading group?'

'A group of people who read a book a month, meet at the home of one of the group to discuss it, and at the end of the evening the next month's book is decided upon. They disperse, read it, meet to discuss it, and so on. That was her only social life that I was able to ascertain. And how popular she was within that group I don't know; certainly no one from the group ever phoned here to contact her. No one phoned to ask after her after she went missing. She received only official-looking letters and only one card at Christmas, with a York postmark. I presume it was from her brother.'

'Her brother cleared her room, I understand?'

'He did. I hardly thought her brother would be like that, her so large yet scrubbed clean, he so small and . . .'

'Yes, I've met him.' Yellich smiled. 'Hygiene isn't high on his list of priorities.' He paused. 'The police would have visited after she was reported missing?'

'Yes, they did. Looked at her room, didn't take anything away.'

'They would have asked you if you knew of her movements when she disappeared, or about the time of same?'

'They did. I couldn't tell them; there was just the invitation to the book-club dinner, which she stuck on her mirror with a bit of Blu-tack. It was there for a week before she disappeared. I took it that the book club had an annual dinner at the house of one of its members. Very spiky handwriting.'

'Do you remember the address?'

'I don't, not after this time, nor the name of the host.'

'Do you know if the book club is still operating?'

'I don't. I don't read, except the newspapers and the magazines, of course.'

'Of course.'

'You could try Pages, in town.'

'Pages?'

'The small independent bookshop, next to the health centre at Precentor's Court. I saw a reading group advertised in the shop window there just the other day. I presume it's the same club.'

'Pages,' Yellich repeated.

Yellich drove back to the city centre and parked his car at the rear of the police station, crossed Micklegate Bar and walked up the steps on to the wall. A slight drizzle fell and the paving flags behind the battlements were glistening with water and tended to be slippery underfoot. A keen breeze blew and seemed to be cutting into his face as he walked the exposed length of the medieval wall to Lendal Bridge. But he knew York, and like all citizens of the famous and Faire he knew that the quickest way to walk from one part of the city centre to another is to 'walk the walls'. Tourists do it for interest, the citizens do it for expediency. He left the walls at Lendal, for the walls are not, as in Chester, continuous, walked across Lendal Bridge, turned right into Lendal, walked past the imposing Judges' Residence and turned left into the narrow confines of Stonegate and then to Precentor's Court, containing two buildings which were both germane to the life of Amanda Dunney. He pondered why George Hennessey had dropped this task in his lap, but he knew Detective Chief Inspector Hennessey and he knew that, whatever the reason, it had to be valid. The bookshop or the health centre? He chose the bookshop.

Inside, the shop was light and airy; brightly coloured displays and dumpbins of books by prominent and/or fashionable writers broke up the floor space like stumpy stalagmites. Posters advertising recently released novels adorned the walls, chamber music played softly in the background, and a spiral staircase beside the counter led, a sign promised, to the gallery and snack bar. Yet despite the colour and music, the bookshop still seemed to Yellich to possess that atmosphere of reverence and solemnity that is found in older, more traditional, bookshops. Books do that to a building or a room: they calm, soothe and soften. It occurred to him then that he had never been called to a 'domestic' involving a house that was full of books. Domestics of varying degrees of violence always occurred, in his experience, in households where video cassettes filled the shelves, or else trinkets from package-tour holiday resorts. He approached the counter and a young girl, a student he thought, working herself through her course, smiled at him. 'Can I help you, sir?'

'Police.' Yellich showed her his ID. 'Can I speak to the manager?'

'Umm . . . I can't leave the counter.'

'Just direct me.'

'Upstairs, through the gallery, the doors ahead of you. I'll let him know you're on your way.' She picked up a brown telephone receiver. Yellich liked the colour, which blended with the shop. He thanked the young girl and walked up the spiral staircase.

'The book club? Or reading group?'

'Ah, yes . . .' The manager revealed himself to be a young man, with a beaming smile and large, proud, square-rimmed spectacles, smartly but casually dressed in an open-neck shirt and brown woollen trousers. Unlike the well-ordered shop, the manager's office was a mess: books stacked haphazardly against the bare, undecorated walls, the phone on his desk covered by pieces of paper. 'The reading group.' He knelt by the electric kettle on the floor of his office which, Yellich noted, afforded a view of a section of a snickelway. 'Would you care for a coffee, or tea?'

'No thanks, I've just had one.' It was an untruth but Yellich thought the chaotic nature of the office boded ill-washed mugs and 'turning' milk.

'As you wish. Do take a pew, if you can find one.'

Yellich couldn't, and remained standing. Back behind his desk the manager, Bill France by the nameplate which peered at Yellich from under a pile of envelopes and letters, blew on his coffee and said, 'Nothing to do with the shop, but we allow the organisers to advertise in here. In return, we ask the members to purchase their books from us. Which they don't. This month they're reading *Dracula* by Bram Stoker.'

Yellich smiled.

'Don't dismiss it. It's a complex, intelligent and multi-layered piece, one discussion group I wouldn't mind being part of. When the title was announced we sold one or two copies of the Penguin edition, but not the twelve we could have hoped for.'

'It's a group of twelve?'

'Twelve maximum, I believe, though the numbers fluctuate. You really need to talk to the organiser.'

'Only if they've been running the group for about fifteen years.'

'I think she has, in fact. The group started when the shop started, and the shop is sixteen years old now.' France clearly saw Yellich's surprise because he added, 'I'm the second manager. The proprietor is getting our second shop off the ground in Leeds.'

'I see.'

France leaned to one side, opened a drawer of his desk and took out a notebook. 'The person you want to speak to is one Mrs Ferguson, Cynthia. I'd prefer to give you her telephone number only, if you don't mind.'

'Fair enough.' Yellich could understand Bill France's reticence but smiled inwardly, courtesy of reverse telephone directories, the police are easily able to match an address to any given telephone number. France recited the number and Yellich scribbled it down on his notepad. He thanked Bill France for his time and information and walked from his office, across a small gallery where modernist sculpture was being displayed and a framed photograph of the artist hung on the wall with a few hundred words of biography beneath the print, through the café, where only one of the six tables was at that moment occupied, down the spiral staircase and out into a drizzly and overcast day. He pulled his coat collar up against the rain and walked the short distance to the health centre.

Inside, the health centre had a similar atmosphere to the bookshop, in that it was quiet and solemn, not a place for levity. It was also brightly decorated and had posters advertising various services pinned to the noticeboard in the waiting room: a gamblers' support group, Alcohol Concern, a domestic-violence advice line, the Childline number. In the waiting room the chairs were arranged in rows, with further chairs round the walls. About a dozen people were waiting patiently. A young child played with a brightly coloured toy; soothing, controlled Radio Four was playing on the radio; a pile of magazines lay disturbed and untidy on a table near to where the child was playing. As was always Yellich's observation, most of the people in the waiting room were women. Men die young, women live for ever, but they live for ever at the expense of indifferent health. There's more going on in a woman's body than there is in a man's, Yellich reasoned, more things to go wrong. Always more female beds in a hospital, always more women in a doctor's waiting room than men. Yellich was happy being a male; he did not at all envy women their lot, save one thing: just once in his life he would like to have experience of the female orgasm − so much longer, so all-consuming, compared to the brief shudder that was the male climax. And after a lot less work too.

'DS Yellich.' Yellich showed his ID to the middle-aged, smartly dressed receptionist. 'Can I see the practice manager, please?'

'I'll see if he's free.' The receptionist picked up the phone on her desk and pressed a two-figure number. 'Police to see you, Mr Pearson,' she said when the call was answered. She listened and said, 'Very good, Mr Pearson.' She replaced the receiver and addressed Yellich. 'If you'd care to go through the swing door, Mr Pearson's office is at the end of the corridor.'

'Diving,' said Pearson as Yellich accepted his invitation to take a seat. Pearson was a smartly dressed man in his fifties.

'Sorry?' Yellich smiled.

'Most people wonder how I broke my back, a few are insensitive enough to ask, but all go away wondering. Whenever you see a fella or a woman in a wheelchair who was clearly born whole, don't you ask yourself, I wonder how he did that?'

'Well, since you mention it . . .'

'I was a young man. I didn't do it from a diving board either, with my head back instead of down. I was in the surf, with my mates, big wave came and I dived into it. I woke up in traction in a hospital, a specialist spinal-injuries unit, hundreds of miles from the candy floss and kiss-me-quick hats. Lost consciousness in one world and woke up in another.'

'I'm sorry.'

'Well, I'm not over the moon about it. My mates didn't notice anything at first, then realised I was floating face-down. They only just revived me from drowning. Confess for many years after I thought, Why did you have to rescue me? Why couldn't you have let me drown?'

'I can understand that, I think.'

'It takes ten years to adjust to a wheelchair. Never know whether it's better to break your back when you're young or when you're middle-aged. With one you have time to adjust and carve some sort of life; with the other at least you've *had* a life; you may have climbed a mountain and become a parent. I'm paralysed at the fifth vertebra, I can move my shoulders, arms, neck – a paraplegic. Any further up and I would have been a quadriplegic, able to speak and that's about all, a brain, eyes and ears stuck to a body that is an inert vegetable.'

'Not funny.'

'No control of bodily functions, so I'm sorry about the smell of urine.'

'It's barely noticeable.'

'Men have it easier than women. You can fit a catheter

tightly round the male member and if I drain the reservoir about once very two hours I can keep on top of the smell. That's why male paraplegics find employment; our wheelchair-bound sisters have to drain into pads and the smell of urine they produce makes it impossible for them to find social acceptance, and hence employment.' Pearson smiled. 'I was dead lucky – or would I have been lucky dead? I can't decide even now. But that's my story, so you won't go away wondering. How can I help the police?'

'Amanda Dunney?'

'Oh . . .' Pearson groaned, 'she haunts us still. Not a clever time for this practice. The confidence of our patients was shaken.'

'Really?' Yellich had already found Pearson to be a very 'giving' personality. He settled back into the chair, knowing that he was going to be told a story.

'Acid-tongued, thin-lipped woman. No longer here. It must be, what? – fifteen years since she left us, soon after I started, and she left well under a cloud. She was suspended, professional malpractice.'

'Can you be specific, Mr Pearson?'

'Well, she was a Roman Catholic, and she allegedly subscribed to the notion of salvation through suffering. In practice what that meant was that she was wilfully under-administering the prescribed dose of morphine to terminally ill patients. It had probably been going on for some time, and she had been getting away with it because the nature of terminal illness is that all of us go there just once, so the patients have no previous experience to draw on. What Dunney was doing was massively under-administering the stuff, so that if the doctor had prescribed, say, thirty units of morphine per day to a patient riddled with cancer who wanted to die at home, Nurse Dunney would visit and administer just ten, and the patient would assume that they were getting all that they were entitled to.'

'Oh.' Yellich felt genuinely dismayed.

'Makes you angry, doesn't it?' Pearson raised his eyebrows. 'It finally came to light when somebody had got prior experience of terminal illness, vicariously speaking. An elderly gentleman had nursed his sister through the final stages of cancer and then he started the whole sad business again with his wife, believing he knew what was going to happen. But he soon noticed that his wife, who he knew wasn't given to complaining, was in much greater distress than his sister had been. He was also a retired chemist and he was able to see at a glance that the amount of morphine in the syringe wasn't anything like the amount the GP had told him would be his wife's daily dose. So he notified the health centre and the doctor told her he would be administering the dose for a number of the terminally ill patients for the next day or two, did so, and asked them how they felt. All reported an absence of pain for the first time in ages and others said they had been able to sleep for the first time for a long while. Dunney was confronted and admitted it. She said, I am told, "They prescribe but I administer."'

'No built-in safeguard.' Yellich was open-mouthed. And angry.

'There isn't, is there? No monitoring. The system is based on the assumption that the nurse will administer the prescribed dose, and on trust that she will. And most abuse is a form of betrayal of trust.'

'It is, isn't it?'

'Well, anyway, Amanda Dunney admitted what she had been doing but claimed it was because of her religious convictions and she genuinely believed she was helping the patients get to heaven more speedily.' There was a note of sarcasm in Pearson's voice.

'You don't sound convinced of that?'

'I'm not. It doesn't gel with Dunney's character as I recall it, to do anything to anybody that could be seen as a kindness, no matter how twisted the logic. I think I can understand her because, unlike the doctors and other nurses, who have been privileged in their life, I have gone occasionally into a state of mind where I wanted a victim. Breaking my back at the age of twenty-two has made me feel bitter, and when I was making my adjustment I found myself doing spiteful things like trapping flies, torturing them to death and enjoying their suffering. I drew pleasure from it. I got good at it, trapping flies, pulling a wing off and then dropping the disabled insect into a spider's web.'

'I can understand that.'

'Can you?'

'I think so.' Yellich pursed his lips. 'A name comes to mind, inservice training . . . Lambrusco?'

Pearson grinned. 'That's a wine. Cesare *Lombroso*, nineteenth-century criminologist, founding father of criminology at Turin University. I did an Open University degree in sociology, which had a criminology component, but yes, you're thinking as I am thinking. The concept that the criminal is also a victim in some way. You can be a victim without also being a criminal, but you can't be a criminal without being a victim. Not necessarily of crime, but some brutalisation, some trauma, some injustice whether real or imagined causes criminality . . . it's all coming back to me now. The injustice of my accident caused me to seek victims, which I found in the form of flies.'

39

'Pretty harmless though.'

'In the scale of things, yes. But had I not dived into that wave, had I completed my degree and begin officer training for the Army . . .'

'Oh, I'm sorry.'

'Yes . . . I had passed the selection board. All I had to do was complete my degree, then I was up to Sandhurst. Took an Easter break with a couple of friends before the final term of the course, just a week in the sun before the last burst of energy and the exams. I was still in traction when they sat their finals. I can't imagine myself as a twenty-five-year-old Army officer making victims out of insects. So the accident changed my personality, and at twenty-five I was living alone in an adapted one-bedroom bungalow, drawing intense pleasure from the death-throes of flies. I used to fry them as well.'

'Flies?'

'Yes. Got skilled at catching them in a tumbler. Invert the tumbler on a frying pan, put a fork from the top of the tumbler to the bottom of the pan so the glass doesn't shatter, apply a low heat . . . the fly doesn't half bounce about. I don't do it any more. I have made my adjustment. I enjoy being good at my job, I have a lovely garden behind my bungalow and a rabbit which I have house-trained. But because of my accident and what it once made me do to flies, I saw something in Amanda Dunney that I don't think anybody else saw.'

'That need for a victim?'

'Exactly. The discussion among the staff here was all focused on how someone could allow her religious values to invade and compromise her professional obligations. But . . . I don't wish to be judgemental, but sometimes you have to be judgemental to grasp the nettle.'

'OK . . . within these four walls. I know she had to

wear maternity smocks all the time, so I can picture her figure.'

'Right, large maternity smocks as well, and not a pleasant face on top of it all. I imagine that any woman dealt that hand in life, who is surrounded by images of female perfection courtesy of the advertising industry, can feel like a victim.'

'And hence, you think, a victim's need for a victim?'

'She had cold eyes, kept making cutting remarks, kept referring to my "next lover" knowing that I haven't had a partner since my accident and am not likely to attract one. But of course she didn't get a partner either.'

'Hence the cutting remarks.'

'As you say.' Pearson shifted his weight from one buttock to the other. 'Have to redistribute my body weight in order to avoid pressure sores. I have no pain warning, you see; my legs could be covered in open sores and I wouldn't know unless I saw them. I have been operated on below the fifth vertebra, intrusive surgery without anaesthetic, all I needed was a plastic cup to vomit in.'

'Sorry to hear that.'

'Oh, there's more to breaking your back than a wheel-chair, Mr Yellich.' This was said with what Yellich thought was a courageous smile. Very courageous.

'Amanda Dunney?' Yellich refocused the conversation.

'She was suspended immediately, and the police were notified. I think they had difficulty framing charges. What she did didn't seem to fit any crime on the statute book. Is withholding medication an assault? It would have been an interesting precedent.'

'Well, it causes pain and distress.' Yellich wondered what other crime she might be construed to have committed.

41

'The patients got to hear about it, and we had angry relatives in here, demanding Dunney's address. A few folk phoned up in a very friendly, calm manner, pretending to be her friend and asking if I could "remind" them of her address. Then she disappeared, just vanished . . . solved a lot of problems in a sense. And now you're asking about her again, after all these years? Has she turned up?'

'Yes.' Yellich saw no reason to hide the information from Pearson; he had warmed to the man and Pearson had given much useful information. 'Her skeleton has.'

'Oh . . .'

'In a field to the north of the city, exposed by flood waters. Over time the course of a beck changed, inched nearer the shallow grave, and the flood waters did the rest. Doubtless you'll hear about it in the media.'

'And it is Amanda?'

'Not definitely – we still have to match the dental records – but it is highly likely to be her.'

'So somebody did get to her. You know, it did cross my mind that that might have happened. There were a lot of angry relatives around at that time. It seems to be the case that people get more annoyed about injuries done to a loved one than injustices done to themselves.'

'I can understand that as well.' Yellich stood. 'Thank you for your information.'

'I'll look them out,' Pearson smiled.

'Look what out?'

'The names and addresses of all the patients Amanda Dunney was helping get to heaven more quickly than the doctors would have wanted. Doubtless you'll want to speak to their relatives?'

Yellich returned the smile. One point to Mr Pearson, he was one step ahead of him. 'Thanks again.'

Yellich walked the walls back to Micklegate Bar Police Station, where he wrote up the interviews with Amanda Dunney's brother, with Mr France and Mr Pearson, adding them to the file of 'Amanda Dunney?'. He felt certain that the question mark would soon be removed. He picked up the phone and dialled the dental surgery.

'If you could show your ID and provide me with a receipt.' Mr Serle had a warm, melodious voice. 'And you'll have to guarantee to return them.'

'Of course, sir,' Yellich assured Serle.

'Well then, I'll look them out. When can you call to pick them up?'

'Soon after lunch, sir.'

'That would be fine.'

Yellich thanked Mr Serle and replaced the telephone receiver.

He took lunch in the canteen. It was inexpensive but filling, not to the taste of the chief inspector, nor of the commander, the presence of either in the canteen being the cause of much comment. But Yellich was a young man, with a needy son, a wife and a mortgage – above all a mortgage – and when his outgoings were as modest as those of the chief inspector and the commander, then he too would lunch out. But until the arrival of those more fortunate times he was obliged to lunch in.

After lunch he picked up the phone, dialled, and when it was answered he identified himself.

'The police?' The voice was alarmed. 'Is anything wrong?'

'Nothing for you to be concerned about, madam. Mr France at the Pages bookshop gave me your number.'

'He did?'

'In connection with a reading group.'

'Oh yes. Do you wish to join us? We have room.'

'No, thank you . . . Can I ask, have you been co-ordinating the club for a while now?'

'How long is a while?' The question was asked with humour. There was also a calm authority to the voice. A retired schoolteacher, perhaps, thought Yellich.

'Since Amanda Dunney was in the group.'

'Amanda . . . Well, that is a name I haven't heard of for some time, and thereby I answer your question.'

'Do you have details of people who were contemporary with Miss Dunney in the group?'

'Details I do not . . . I don't keep records. Any telephone numbers would be in my personal address book. I changed my address book three years ago, about, and only transferred the address from the old book to the new if I was still in contact with the person concerned. Amanda's name was not transferred.'

'I see. Did Miss Dunney have any particular friends in the reading group?'

'I don't think so. She wasn't . . . well, particularly popular. She was suffered more than she was accepted and her presence wasn't eagerly sought.'

'She did receive an invitation to the reading group annual dinner though?'

'She did not!'

'Not invited?'

'No.'

'I see. Not popular, as you say, Mrs Ferguson.'

'Not a question of popularity, Mr . . . ?'

'Yellich.'

'Yellich. Not a question of popularity. The reading group does not have an annual dinner.'

Yellich paused. 'It doesn't?'

'That's what I said.'

'Oh . . .' Yellich paused. He glanced out of his office

window. The sky was darkening; a rainstorm was in the offing. 'Who was contemporary with her in the group before she disappeared?'

'Before?'

'I mean about the time of her disappearance.'

'That's a more sensible question, I would have thought.'

'Well . . . Major Robertson and Timothy Ashton, the retired classicist, were, but they are now both deceased. Sandra Da Silva has gone to live in New Zealand with her second husband; Thomas Ryden is still in the group, he was a contemporary of Amanda's. He's a bachelor, a chartered accountant, quite a catch for a woman like Amanda, but he made it plain he wasn't interested in her. She would come on to him embarrassingly strongly. It was a reading group, not a dating agency. Mrs Vesty is still in the group: she was a contemporary of Amanda's, as was Martin Mason. Nobody else is still in the group who would have known Amanda. Other people have joined subsequently.'

'So, just four,' Yellich pondered. 'Thomas Ryan, the chartered accountant, whom Amanda liked but who didn't care for her; a Mrs Vesty—'

'Who didn't have anything to do with Amanda, I may say.'

'What about Martin Mason?'

'Headmaster of Sentinel Lane Primary School. Lovely man. That's three.'

'And yourself, Mrs Ferguson.'

'Myself?'

'You're the fourth person who knew Amanda socially about the time of her disappearance.'

'I suppose I was, yes. Why the belated interest? Has she turned up?'

'In a manner of speaking, yes, she has. Can you please

let me have the telephone numbers of the other three people?'

'I don't know if I should. I prefer to ask them to phone you.'

'I could get a court order to force you to release this information.'

'Oh well, in that case. I'll have to go to the study for my address book, but I insist on phoning you back with the information.'

A few moments later Yellich was in possession of all three telephone numbers. He added the names and numbers to the file under the heading 'Amanda Dunney's Social Circle'.

He placed the file neatly in the drawer of the grey Home Office filing cabinet which stood in the corner of his office. He then glanced out of his window again and tried to read the weather. The rain seemed to be holding off. Gillygate was on the route to York City Hospital. It seemed such a lazy thing to do to drive the short distance from Micklegate Bar to Gillygate and Mr Serle's dental practice, and then on to the York City Hospital. He decided to walk. Besides, he thought as he signed out at the enquiry desk, the walk would give him a little 'space'. A busy man needs all the space he can get.

'I think it's safe to assume that there will be a match.' George Hennessey ran a liver-spotted hand through his silver hair. 'The dental records will show the skull to be that of Amanda Dunney.' He reached forward, picked up the mug of coffee and sipped.

'I think so too, boss.' Yellich sat in front of Hennessey's desk, his left ankle resting on his right leg. He too sipped a mug of coffee.

'And you suspect her social circle, rather than angered relatives of her unfortunate patients?'

'Yes, I do. You see, if Sarah died in needless agony because of Nurse Dunney, I would be angry. I can well understand the relatives of her patients besieging the health centre wanting her address, if not her blood, but would it lead to murder and the burial of her body in a shallow grave in a field? I think not.'

'I'm sympathetic, but not wholly swayed. I don't think we should lose sight of the possibility that the culprit is an angered relative. But go on.'

'That speaks of premeditated murder, and for that you're looking at a relationship of some sort. The relatives of her patients would be content to know that she was finished as a nurse, no more employment for her anywhere, loss of pension. That would satisfy me once my anger had left me, if Sarah had been one of her "victims" (I can hardly call them patients). So we have the members of the reading group, her landlady and her brother. Of the three, my feeling is that the culprit is a member of the reading group. Two men and a woman are still with us; two other men are now deceased and another woman has gone to live in New Zealand. The one thing that does puzzle me is that her landlady recalls her receiving an invitation to a reading-group annual dinner, but the organiser of the group tells me that the group had no such dinner.'

'Interesting, but let's keep an open mind. What do you intend to do?'

'I'll go back and ask her what she can remember about it – the invitation, I mean.'

'Yes . . . It may be something but it may also be nothing, a complete blind alley.'

'Will do, boss, I'll call on her tomorrow.'

'So you paint a picture of Amanda Dunney as a lonely, possibly embittered woman, given to cheap, cutting remarks, unable to attract a partner, who by some twisted reasoning abused the trust placed in her to cause people intense pain?'

'Yes.' Yellich nodded. 'That's the picture which came across. Not a woman I would want to meet.'

'This is why I asked you to find out what you can about her, because there is information that I have withheld from you.'

'Oh?' Yellich said with a smile.

'Yes. The post-mortem threw up information which didn't gel with the picture of Nurse Dunney as given in the missing-persons report, to wit that she was a fifty-three-year-old spinster.'

'Yes . . . ?'

'The skeleton in the grave is that of a woman who had given birth—'

Yellich's jaw sagged. 'I didn't know you could tell that from a skeleton.'

'Apparently you can – it's something called "pubic scarring" – but Dr D'Acre was certain: not just one birth, but many.'

'The impression of Nurse Dunney is that she never had a partner, let alone experienced pregnancy and parenthood.'

'So we must have the skeletal remains of not one, but two women. The skull of one, the rest belonging to another, but definitely in the same grave, of similar age when they died.'

'Someone putting us off the scent, do you think, boss?'

'Has to be. Someone anticipating that the grave might be found, and wanting us to believe we had found the body of Nurse Dunney. And we probably would have fallen for it, had not the expert eye of Dr D'Acre noticed the pubic scarring.'

Yellich sat back in his chair. 'Wow!' It was the only thing he could think of to say.

'"Wow" indeed. Somebody wanted the other lady dead more than they wanted Amanda Dunney dead. The other body had a family; she would be noticed missing more quickly than Nurse Dunney.'

'But not from this area, boss, otherwise our mis-per files would have a record of it.'

'My thinking entirely. Have to scan the nationwide database. Perhaps you could ask the collator to set that in motion before you leave for the day. Should have the results waiting for you to address tomorrow morning. Someone alien to York, but who, when she died, might have had a connection with the city.'

'Right, boss.' Yellich stood. 'You won't be in tomorrow then?'

'Not me. Weekend off. A rare luxury, even for chief inspectors.'

'Doing anything?'

'No.' Hennessey drank the now cool coffee. 'Nothing special.'

Three

*In which a middle-aged couple play a game and
Detective Sergeant Yellich has occasion to visit
Humberside*

FRIDAY EVENING 1 APRIL–SATURDAY 2 APRIL

George Hennessey left the police station at 5 p.m.
He was held up in the rush-hour traffic but none
the less was pleased to have reached Easingwold and his
house on Thirsk Road by 5.45. He let himself in and
was warmly greeted by his brown mongrel. He picked
up the mail delivered that morning after he had left for
work: bills, junk mail and a postcard from his son from
Middlesbrough, 'Just', as he had written on the reverse,
'for the hell of it!'

Hennessey went upstairs and changed out of his suit
into more comfortable trousers and casual shirt and jacket,
packed a bag for two nights, plus walking boots and water-
proofs, then set the timer switches for the security lights in
the upstairs and downstairs of his house. He carried the
bag and hiking gear out to his car and returned for Oscar
and Oscar's food and water bowls. Then he drove away,
with Oscar sitting beside him, staring steadfastly out of
the windscreen.

He drove north to Thirsk, where he turned westwards,
driving through country which he found pleasant to the

eye. He crossed over the A1 on to the B6267, which he followed to Masham, and to the car park of the Rose and Crown. Leaving Oscar in the car, he entered the hotel and walked up to the reception desk. The interior of the hotel he found instantly comforting: dark-coloured carpets, low black beams and a wood fire crackling in the hearth opposite the reception desk. Pamphlets of local tourist attractions stood at the side of the desk and while waiting to be attended to he selected one about the Embsay Light Railway. Having travelled on the North Yorkshire Moors Steam Railway and (many times) on the Worth Valley Steam Railway, with the near-obligatory walk up the steep cobbled hill at Haworth to visit the Parsonage, it left only the Embsay Light Railway to 'knock off'. Then he would have travelled on all the local steam-preservation lines, enjoying the magic of steam locomotion, the animal movement of the engines, the smell of the steam.

'Good-evening, sir.' The receptionist was a young woman whose manner and appearance caused Hennessey to warm to her. 'Can I help you?'

'George Hennessey. I have a single room booked for tonight and tomorrow.'

'Ah, yes . . .' The receptionist consulted the register. 'From Easingwold. Not a long journey for you, sir?'

'All that's needed for a pleasant change of atmosphere and surroundings, do a bit of walking, get up on the hills, really clear the tubes.'

'I know what you mean, sir. How will you be paying for the room?'

'Credit card?'

'Excellent . . . If I could have the card, please.'

Hennessey was given the key to room number seven, and he carried his bag up the carpeted stairway, the wood-panelled walls smelling strongly of furniture polish.

Fearful of making a dreadful error, he tapped on the door of room seven before unlocking it and entering. The first thing he noticed was the size of the bed, a double, then he checked the wardrobe, drawers and bathroom. He returned downstairs to the reception desk. Dinner, he was told, would be served up until nine o'clock. He walked into the lounge bar, which was similarly thickly carpeted, and low-beamed with a log fire. Three other guests were there, a young, professional-looking couple sitting at a table in the corner, leaning towards each other, not interested in anybody or anything save each other. The third guest was a slender woman with short, dark hair, in her forties, Hennessey thought, smartly dressed in a grey suit and patent-leather shoes, sitting in front of a glass of colourless liquid, probably, thought Hennessey, a white wine. She was reading a copy of *Yorkshire Life*. She glanced up once as George Hennessey entered the room, then returned her attention to the magazine. A quiet country hotel for the weekend. Just what the doctor ordered.

Hennessey left the hotel building and walked to the car park, collected Oscar and waited patiently while his dog wolfed his supper and then drank deeply from the water bowl, which Hennessey had filled from a plastic bottle brought from home. Then he took Oscar for a long walk. He left Oscar in the car for the night, one window slightly open and on one of Hennessey's old shirts for familiarity and reassurance.

He went to his room, washed and changed his shirt, and went to the lounge bar. The couple were still in the corner; the elegantly dressed lady was still engrossed in her magazine, though her glass was empty. Hennessey glanced at her fingers and was surprised that such a clearly accomplished and attractive woman wore no rings at all, though she did have a gold bracelet on one wrist and a gold watch on the other.

'Yes, sir.' The attentiveness of the barman, a young man in a white shirt, black bow tie and black trousers, drew Hennessey's attention from the woman.

'Whisky, please.'

'Yes, sir. We have Bell's, Whyte and Mackay, Teacher's, Regal . . .'

'Oh, Bell's, thank you. I don't have the Scotsman's educated taste in whisky.'

Suddenly Hennessey was aware of the elegantly dressed woman standing beside him.

'Yes, madam?'

'Another white wine, please.' She had a soft voice, yet a voice of authority, the self-assuredness that comes from learning.

Hennessey turned to her, 'Would you allow me, madam?'

The woman looked at him, but demurely so, paused and then said, 'Thank you, sir, that would be most kind.'

'White wine for the lady, please.' Hennessey addressed the barman.

'Yes, sir. Dry, wasn't it, madam?'

'It was. Thank you.' She turned to Hennessey. 'Perhaps you'd care to join me?'

'I wouldn't be intruding on anything?'

'Not at all. Frankly I would enjoy the company. I'm having a weekend away, just for myself, by myself.'

'Strange you should say that.' Hennessey paid for the drinks and enjoyed the slight, generously good-humoured smile of the young barman.

Over drinks Hennessey learned that the woman was a divorcee, had three teenage children (with their father that weekend) and was a doctor.

'I'm a police officer,' he said, 'widowed.'

'Oh, I'm sorry.'

'Long time ago now.'

'Even so . . .'

'Well . . . have you eaten?'

'Not yet.'

'Well, perhaps you'd care to join me for dinner.'

'Thank you, but I insist on paying for myself.'

'As you wish.' Hennessey walked to the bar and asked for two copies of the menu. Again smiling warmly, the barman handed the menus to Hennessey.

'I can take your order, sir. I'll come over for it.'

'Good. Give us ten minutes. Thank you.'

They were offered a table in the corner of the dining room and served faultlessly by a smiling waitress who seemed to be happy for them. For their meal, they selected different first courses, but both chose venison for the main course, which was, they agreed, excellent. It was finished by a round of Irish coffee.

'I shall sleep well tonight,' the woman said.

'So shall I. This hotel is quite near my home. I live in Easingwold, but it could be . . . it could be a different country.'

'Same here. As I said, I live in York, and you're right, it could be a different country.' She stood, Hennessey likewise. 'Thank you for an enjoyable evening, Mr Hennessey.'

'I thoroughly enjoyed it.'

'Good-night.'

The murderer, unlike George Hennessey and his lady companion, did not eat that cold, rainy Friday evening. He did not feel hungry, not at all. He lay in his bed, listening to the rain patter on the window pane, and thought that the secret, the secret now was to do nothing, nothing that he wouldn't normally do. So they had found the bodies, both of them. The great lie that was his life would soon be exposed – unless . . . unless he could continue to act normally, until the police investigation fizzled out and police time was given to more recent crimes. *Act normally*, he told himself, *just act normally*, as *though nothing has happened*. None he less, sleep evaded him that night.

George Hennessey had slept well, an unusually good night's rest because he usually had difficulty sleeping for the first night in a strange bed. He had lain there, thinking about the day, planning tomorrow, but he could not help his thoughts returning to the slender, graceful woman who had been his dinner companion.

He woke early on the Saturday morning and enjoyed a long bath, then dressed and went out to the car park to allow Oscar to run around for a few minutes, which he did, criss-crossing the car park as the day before he had criss-crossed the lawn at the rear of George Hennessey's house.

The woman was already at her breakfast when Hennessey entered the dining room. They nodded to each other briefly and Hennessey sat at a separate table. A cooked breakfast, especially when cooked by someone else, was by far his favourite meal. He ate leisurely, that morning's copy of the *Guardian* propped up in front of him.

Hennessey and the woman met again later that morning. He had changed into his walking clothes: a solid pair of walking boots, socks, corduroy trousers, a full-length waterproof, a tweed hat. He went to the reception desk to hand his key to the smiling receptionist and when he was there the woman approached, also to hand in her key, also dressed for the hills.

55

'You're going for a walk today?' Hennessey asked.

The woman smiled and indicated her clothing.

'Yes . . . bit of a silly question.' Hennessey laid his key on the desk. It was swept up by the receptionist, who continued to lean forward, head slightly bowed.

'Actually, I'm not going for a walk.'

'You're not?'

'No, Mr Hennessey. I walk to the shops sometimes. I'm actually going for a hike or a ramble, but "a walk" somehow doesn't convey the sort of journey I envisage making.' She too laid her key on the counter. It was picked up by the receptionist, who still made no move to place the keys in the corresponding pigeonholes.

'Where do you intend to go, may I ask?'

'You may. On a hill – any hill that promises fresh air and a little solitude, ideal for a lady who gets too little of either.'

'Well, you are welcome to join my friend and me, if you wish, and if you don't want absolute solitude.'

'Oh.' The woman looked crestfallen. 'I'm sorry, I didn't realise you had a partner.'

'Constant and faithful.' Hennessey stole a glance at the receptionist and saw the woman smiling what seemed to be a genuine I'm-happy-for-you smile, one which seemed to vanish when Hennessey made reference to his 'friend', but which returned again when Hennessey said, 'To wit, one brown mongrel, Oscar by name.'

'I love dogs.' The woman smiled. 'I have a horse.'

'Oh, really? I don't know horses.' Hennessey walked towards the hotel doorway.

'Well, I warn you' – the woman fell into step beside him – 'one gallop and you're hooked. But it's a mighty expensive pastime.'

'Had a friend once' – Hennessey held the door open

for her – 'he used to be a keen sailor, a yachtsman. He described the sport as like standing under a cold shower tearing up twenty-pound notes.'

The woman smiled. 'Horse riding is a bit like that; the bumpiest ride of your life, the coldest, the windiest, and as you canter along, as you say, you pull twenty-pound notes out of your pocket and toss them aside. Where's your dog?'

'In the car park. He sleeps in the car.'

As they walked along the pavement to the car park at the side of the hotel Hennessey said, 'Well, so far so good.'

'Definitely got their interest,' said Louise D'Acre.

Yellich listened with amusement as a young and clearly exasperated constable tried to give directions to a tourist.

'Then left . . .'

'Leeft?' The olive-skinned tourist pointed to his right hand. 'This is leeft, sir?'

'No, sir, that is right.' The constable pointed to the man's other hand. 'That is left.'

'Leeft?' The man pointed to his left hand.

'Sir . . . I mean yes, sir, that is left, left . . . Turn left.'

Yellich smiled to himself and walked to the CID corridor, leaving the constable to struggle and to learn to cope with his exasperation. In his pigeonhole was the result of the nationwide details of women in their forties who were reported missing between twelve and fifteen years ago. Twenty-five of them. Yellich took the computer print-out to his desk, made a mug of coffee – without which his mind would not function, at least before midday – and scanned the list. All parts of the British Isles seemed to be represented, but none had a York connection. He sipped the coffee. He didn't think he could dismiss any of the names, but he might, he thought, just might be able to narrow the list down. It was, he felt, if the skull belonged to one woman and the body to another, reasonable to assume that both women had disappeared at the same time. If bits of the two women were placed in the same hole, then it was likely that the bits were placed there at the same time. Amanda Dunney was reported missing in September twelve years ago. Of the twenty-five names, only two were reported missing at the same time, within a week of Amanda Dunney being reported as a 'mis-per'. And both just prior to Amanda Dunney, which, if she was murdered to form a smokescreen for another murder, would make sense. Murder the woman you want to murder, then murder Amanda Dunney for her skull and her teeth so as to mislead by dental records.

The first woman's home address was given as Bridgnorth, Shropshire. She had been reported missing by her husband, one Nigel Cox. Mrs Marian Cox was a schoolteacher; 'she had had no known reason to leave her family, especially so close to the start of the school year' was all the computer print-out told Yellich.

The other woman seemed altogether more promising. She had an address in the city of Kingston-upon-Hull, shortened by all for convenience, even on its railway-station nameplates, to 'Hull', which was really the name of a small tributary of the mighty Humber. Calling the city Hull was, Yellich often thought, akin to calling London 'Fleet' because of the tributary of the Thames of that name. Yellich was not unfamiliar with Hull. He found it a hard city; its status as a seaport saw to that. It was also very windy – its proximity to the North Sea saw to that – nor was it a financially successful city. The last time he had visited he had observed boarded-up shop units in the city centre. But he had met one or two folk from Hull who loved the town, who wouldn't hear anything said against it, and who missed the wind when they visited inland cities. It was not, he said to himself, for him to judge. None the less, a visit to Kingston-upon-Hull seemed to be in the offing: one Amy Lepping, who was in her forties, had disappeared from her home in Hull a few days before Amanda Dunney had been reported missing from her lodgings. Mrs Lepping was reported missing by her husband, whose occupation was given as 'farm manager'. Hull was only an hour's drive from York, and a farm manager could read a rural landscape better than most men: he could identify a pasture that was not likely to be dug up. A pasture on a derelict farm, close to a river, for example. He put the computer print-out down, phoned Precentor's Court Health Centre and asked to be put through to the practice manager.

'Pearson.' His manner was brisk, efficient.

'DS Yellich, I called on you yesterday. Didn't think you'd be working on Saturday morning, thought I'd take a chance.'

'I don't usually, but the surgery is open on Saturday mornings and I have some admin to catch up on.'

'The names you said you'd look up for us . . . ?'

'Bit early in the piece. I'll need more time than this.'

'Appreciate that, Mr Pearson, but we have had a couple of possible names fed to us, possibly in respect of another incident. I wondered if the names meant anything to you in respect of Amanda Dunney's patients?'

'Or her victims.'

'As you say. It would be better if you could give me what names you have had time to identify. I presume you are going back to her patient list at the time?'

'Yes, that's all I can do. Really there are not many,

because not all her patients were terminally ill of course; only those who were terminally ill became victims of her twisted ethos.'

'Of course.' Yellich glanced out of his office window; a sliver of blue rent the grey sky.

'Stayed late last night, really didn't know how far to go back, but working backwards from the time she was suspended for eighteen months, I found five names, I think . . . I have the list here somewhere . . . Yes, here we are . . . To get the full, complete list of her victims—'

'You're angry with her, aren't you?'

'Yes, that's why I prefer to refer to her patients as "victims". You see, she did not just betray her patients, she betrayed her colleagues and the nursing profession in general. So yes, I am angry. That woman betrayed me and everybody who works in this practice in any capacity.'

'I can appreciate your anger. A corrupt police officer in this nick would make me feel betrayed.'

'So, the names . . . Giles, Mark; Blackburn, Emily; Lepping, Sara, without an "h"; Mulholland, Deirdre; and Calley, Edith. Those were the terminally ill patients on that woman's patient list for the last eighteen months of her employment with us, but she was here for a number of years, so I'll go back until she started here. That'll take a day or two.'

'It's enough to be going on with, Mr Pearson.' Yellich shifted the phone from one ear to the other. 'Can you tell me anything about the patients?'

'Only what's on the screen when I type in their name.'

'I see. Well, Sara Lepping, what can you tell me about her?'

'Just a second.' The receiver was laid on the desk and Yellich heard the unmistakable hollow sound of a computer keyboard being tapped, speedily and efficiently.

The receiver was picked up again, Pearson sighed and said, 'OK, she's up on the screen now . . . Oh dear . . .'

'What's that?'

'A tragedy: cancer of the ovaries, but she was only twenty years old.'

'Oh.'

'There's no rhyme or reason to it all.'

'There isn't, is there?'

'But twenty years, a miss – single lady – occupation is given as "student", next of kin her father, an address in Humberside: Hedon, Tapping Lane, number seven. She'd left home, didn't return to die there.'

'Stubbornly independent?'

'Or home was so awful she refused to return. One or the other.'

'Well, thanks, that's been a good help.'

It had been a pleasant walk. It was one of the walks that George Hennessey knew he would take with him for the remainder of his life. He and his two companions had driven from Masham to a little way beyond the village of Healey, where they had parked the car and had walked the reservoirs, doing a figure of eight round Leighton Reservoir and its smaller neighbour, Roundhill, a pleasant ten miles, approximated George Hennessey, in remote, rough moorland landscape; up on the way out and downhill on the way back. A late pub lunch in Healey and all in good walking weather, a little wind, comfortably above freezing, and no rain. They returned to the hotel and, leaving Oscar in the car, they entered the hotel, one behind the other but as a couple, and asked for their room keys. The receptionist, a different woman from the receptionist who was on duty when they had left that morning, welcomed them with a knowing smile.

The receptionist had clearly been told of them: the game was working.

'Most pleasant walk.' Hennessey picked up his key. 'Thank you for your company.'

'Thank you for yours. It wouldn't have been half so much fun if I had spent the morning by myself as I had planned.'

'Well . . .' Hennessey hesitated. 'I don't wish to be forward, but would you care to join me for dinner again this evening?'

'Only if you would join me in my trip to Harrogate.'

'This afternoon?'

'Yes. I'm told it's good for antique shops, and I want a dresser for my daughter's bedroom.'

'I'd like that . . . haven't been to Harrogate for years.'

'You know the town?'

'A little.'

'Enough to know where the antique shops are?'

'And the teashops too.'

'I'll see you just here then, give ourselves a chance to get out of our "walkies" . . . about half an hour?'

'Half an hour it is.' Hennessey smiled, and from the corner of his eye noticed the receptionist being barely able to conceal her amusement.

Yellich replaced the receiver and pondered his next move. The man Lepping was clearly a man to be met, a man with a motive to harm Amanda Dunney, a man whose wife also disappeared at the time of Amanda Dunney's disappearance. It was at times like this that he felt the absence of a senior officer, but he knew the investigation must not be allowed to lose momentum. He was also keenly aware that his next board would be strongly influenced by evidence of his ability to act on his own initiative. On that basis, he thought, Humberside beckoned, and the first port of call would be to the Humberside Police, a courtesy call and a request for any local knowledge about Lepping esquire.

'I checked with Directory Enquiries.' Yellich extended his hand and accepted the mug of coffee from the duty CID officer of the Humberside Police. It had taken him just one hour to drive to Hull, across flat wolds landscape, and, as on earlier occasions when entering Hull, he had the sensation of driving down into something. But he didn't like the south of England any better: life in the south seemed so soft to him that he always felt that he was cheating, somehow. All it meant, he decided as he picked his way along Anlaby Road, amongst slow-moving traffic, was that in Great Britain, with all its rich variety within such a small island, he had found the few square miles where he felt at home and content. 'So I came here, only had to ask directions once.'

'You don't know Hull?'

'Not well. I am intrigued by a street called The Land of Green Ginger.'

'Oh, yes, it's in the Old Town, the museums are down that way.' Detective Sergeant Pippa Booth was, thought Yellich, a perfect example of the often made observation that when the Vikings eventually left this part of England they just didn't leave place names behind but their genes as well. 'Hedon has a historical claim to fame too.'

'Oh?'

'Had an outbreak of cholera there in the nineteenth century, lost a lot of folk, more per capita than the city of Hull. It was before they knew what caused the disease, and folk pointed to it as proof that cholera was airborne. How else could the disease reach Hedon unless it was carried on the wind? In fact we now know it was caused by a combination of a near-drought and a low fall.'

'Fall?'

'The inclining of the drains to the river.'

'I see.'

'The drains just dried up and the human waste from the privies seeped into the soil and contaminated the well.'

'Fascinating.'

There was a knock on the door. DS Booth said, 'Yes?' The door opened and a young, eager-looking constable entered holding a file.

'The file you asked for, sarge.'

'Many thanks.' Pippa Booth accepted the file with a gracious, well-mannered smile. 'So . . .' she said as the constable left the room, closing the door gently behind him, 'the file on Sydney Lepping, no less.'

'Slender,' Yellich observed.

'Clearly not a bad lad, by comparison.' Pippa Booth opened the file. 'Well, all happened in the last ten years, nothing known of him before that. It appears to be all drink-related: breach of the peace . . . drink-driving . . . driving whilst disqualified . . . assault . . . then nothing for the last five years. Seems to have calmed down, or maybe he is no longer with us, one of the two. Last address is given as Wickersley Avenue, number fifty-seven. There's reference here to the reason for your visit, his wife's disappearance. The mis-per report is in the void, but all information is duplicated here. The wife, Amy Lepping, née Martin, was reported missing shortly after the death of their daughter, Sara.'

'Yes, she was a student at York, cancer.'

'Oh . . .'

'Yes, tragic isn't it?'

'So he lost his wife and daughter within a few weeks of each other. No mention of any other relative that might give the man reason to continue with this life.'

Pippa Booth scanned the file. 'His first occupation was given as "farm manager", but at his last offence he was listed as "unemployed", the inference being that he lost his job because of his offending or drinking – possibly the latter. A sudden drink problem late in life can lead to absenteeism in a man who was previously a good worker. And now you suspect him of murder?'

'He's *a* suspect, one of a few. Many people had a motive to murder Amanda Dunney.'

'I should think they did. Withholding morphine so they'd get to heaven more quickly, I have never heard the like. Nonsense as well, if you ask me. I may have been a cop for too long but I see that as a thin excuse for a spiteful and sadistic form of pleasure-taking.'

'The practice manager is of the same opinion. He has little time for her memory.'

'Pity she didn't live long enough to experience the pain of cancer herself, that would have changed her mind. Not much salvation in that form of suffering. Yes, I can see why Lepping would be a prime suspect all right. He's a man with a violent streak, according to his track.' Pippa Booth tapped the file. 'And a skeleton of A. N. Other woman was found with Amanda Dunney's skull, you say? I wonder if Dunney knew her name meant "toilet" in some circles. Seems appropriate in a way.'

'Never heard that.' Yellich smiled.

'I think Aussies use the term, and the Kiwis as well, and it was used in these parts until recently. My father grew up on a farm just to the north of Hull and he recalls a two-person outside toilet – two people could sit side by side, you see – which he referred to as a "two-man dunney". Well, to continue, the bits of the other woman are those of a woman who was aged mid-forties when she died, found in the same hole in the ground as Amanda

Dunney's skull, who was reported missing at about the same time that Mrs Amy Lepping was reported missing. Do you intend to arrest Lepping?'

'If he's still with us, as you say, but I don't know. At the moment I think I want to take the measure of the man, feel my way forward.'

'Proceed with caution, you think?'

'I think so, that's the ticket.'

'I think I'd like to come with you. If the body is that of Mrs Lepping it's one for us anyway. Would you mind?'

'Not at all. It would be my pleasure.'

'And it would get me out.' Pippa Booth reached for her handbag. 'Had a loathsome encounter this morning, ugh. Makes me want to have a shower.'

'Oh?' Yellich stood.

'A hardened criminal, from a family of hardened criminals. And he's still not a teenager. Lot of bag-snatching in Hull, elderly women in the main, all describe a little lad that tears along the pavement like a mini-tornado, powers into them, snatches their bag and tears away. About twenty incidents. Today we caught him; a couple of plain-clothes boys saw everything and he ran into them.'

'Good for them.'

'But . . .' Pippa Booth smiled and raised a finger. 'He gives up without a struggle and admits to stealing the one bag the police saw him steal, because his dad had told him to give up without a fight if he was caught bang to rights, and admit to what he can't get out of, but otherwise "cough to nowt". So we lean on him, hard-cop soft-cop routine, a social worker in the room as the law dictates, but would he cough? Would he ever. He was harder than all three adults put together. All we could do was charge him with the one incident. After the tape recorder was switched off and the social worker was about to take him away to a lovely warm children's home—'

'From which he'll abscond.'

'Of course, goes without saying. Anyway, he said, win some lose some, get caught, get away with it, but get away with more than you get caught for, that way you come out on top. His dad told him that as well.'

'Blimey, and how old is he, twelve?'

'Nine. He's nine years old.'

Hennessey and D'Acre drove to Harrogate. The day remained overcast with a little intermittent rain. Hennessey parked near the station and he and Louise D'Acre strolled arm-in-arm round the spa town with its graceful Victorian buildings, wide streets, massively generous 'Stray' – a cultivated, grassed-over area in the centre of the town, criss-crossed by tree-lined roads. They walked, as they had intended, from one antique shop to another but, not being able to find a dresser to Louise D'Acre's liking, or price range, abandoned the search in favour of a window table in a tearoom, a pot of Earl Grey and a 'Yorkshire fat rascal' each.

'Well, yours or mine?' Louise D'Acre ate the last morsel of her 'fat rascal' and patted her lips with the napkin.

Hennessey grinned. 'Whose bed did we use last time?'

'Mine.'

'Did we?'

'Yes, the hotel in Buxton. You remember, the baking hot day. My Riley overheated on the drive back to York.'

'Oh yes, of course. It was a long time ago. Last summer.'

'Quite a good one that; the hotel staff could barely contain their mirth.'

'I remember, they were mostly very young. I think they were amused that people of our age can still have romantic encounters.'

'What joys await them.'

'Indeed. They reminded me of the young female assistant I bought some massage oil from – she clearly couldn't believe that someone old enough to be her grandfather would want to smooth that stuff all over someone else's body.'

'She doesn't know what she's missing. You do it so well; you know the value of taking your time.'

Hennessey smiled. 'This lot have cottoned on all right, I think this is going to be a good one.'

'I think so too. Better than that awful hotel outside Manchester.'

'Oh, horrible, they were brain-dead. You know, when I came up north, I was told that I'd come across the Yorkshire–Lancashire rivalry. In fact I haven't – not as much as I thought I would – but one bloke told me that, and I quote, "All Lancashire folk are Yorkshire folk who've had their brains removed."'

Louise D'Acre smiled, but not at the joke, but because she saw warmth and happiness in George Hennessey's eyes, where mostly she saw only wounding and wisdom. 'But when I think of that hotel staff, I think I know what he meant. No reaction at all. You'd think all their guests all arrived as singles and left in partnerships.'

'That's the problem with the game: we have to use a different hotel each time, we can't find a good one and keep returning. So, your room or my room tonight?'

'Lady's choice.'

'Your room then. That way I get to sleep in both rooms and you only get to sleep in the one.'

Hennessey slid his hand across the table, took her hand and gently, lovingly, squeezed it.

Pippa Booth drove out of Hull and across the flat landscape to Hedon. Yellich saw it to be a town with a mixture of prosperous-looking new-build housing estates and of older terrace housing which lined the main road, complete with its white-painted telephone boxes, unique in Britain, belonging to the Hull Telecommunications Company. He was particularly taken with the Holy Trinity Church, which stood on the only elevated ground in the vicinity, so far as Yellich could tell, and which Pippa Booth informed him was known as 'the King of Holderness' to distinguish it from another church in the area known as 'the Queen of Holderness'.

Wickersley Avenue revealed itself to be a short road of council houses, one boarded up, another with a splintered front door, all with unkempt gardens.

'Happy about leaving your car here?' Yellich turned to Pippa Booth.

'No . . . I think you're right.' She halted and reversed back to the main road and found a parking space amongst other cars outside a small shopping centre. An unemployed youth and several surly-looking children eyed Booth and Yellich with suspicion and dislike.

'I wish we didn't have "Police" written on our foreheads.' Pippa Booth smiled as she locked the car and Yellich found he enjoyed her sense of humour. He enjoyed the company of DS Booth and could well understand the wedding ring on her finger.

The two officers walked back to Wickersley Avenue and found number 57, last known address of Lepping, Sydney, one-time farm manager, last recorded as being unemployed. Number 57 merged well with the other houses in Wickersley Avenue, in Yellich's view. The front garden was overgrown; piles of domestic refuse had been allowed to accumulate by the side of the house. Once in bin liners, as required, it was now scattered, the bin liners having doubtless been torn open by dogs or foxes. The smell from the house was overpowering.

Inside it was worse. Much worse. Sydney Lepping flung open the door at Yellich's distinct *tap, tap . . . tap*, soft but authoritative police officer's knock. Lepping was barefoot, clad in unwashed, inexpensive denim and a vest; his hair was matted; his chin had two or three days' growth; his eyes burned with anger. 'What?'

'Police.' Yellich and Booth showed their IDs.

'I know. I can tell coppers. I knew you were coppers when I heard your car, when you drove up the street and reversed it away again. Coppers would know what'd happen to their car if they left it in this street. Nowhere is safe round here, not for a copper's car, not even where you left it.'

'How do you know where we left it?'

'You left it within two minutes' walk. You'll have had to leave it further away than that to have something to come back to.' Lepping smiled. It was a sneer of joy at the thought of what would be happening to the officers' car.

'We'll take the risk.' Booth's attitude was cold, distant. 'It's not my car anyway; any repairs won't come out of my pocket.'

Lepping stopped sneering.

Yellich understood why the man's daughter didn't want to die at home.

'So what do you want?' He was a strongly built man; he had a farmer's hands, large, paw-like.

'We'd like to ask you a few questions, Mr Lepping.'

'About?'

'About your wife.'

'She walked out on me.'

'And about a lady called Amanda Dunney.'

'That cow. What about them?'

'Be better inside?'

Lepping glanced at the officers and stood his ground.

'We could do it at the police station. We'll take you there but we won't bring you back.'

'It's a long walk from Hull, and it's too cold for an enjoyable walk,' Yellich added.

Lepping continued to stand his ground. Then he suddenly withdrew, turned his back on the officers and walked into his house, leaving the door open. Yellich and Booth interpreted it as an invitation to enter, and followed him inside.

Lepping's manner changed. He became calm, resigned. He sank into an armchair and, far from looking aggressively at Booth and Yellich, he seemed to have a defeated look in his eyes. 'I'd stand up if I were you. Most visitors do, the one or two I get each year. I never did get the hang of housework.'

'We've been in worse.' Yellich walked to the centre of the room; as he did so his feet stuck to the carpet and he easily imagined small things, very small things, running up his trouser-legs. Even his scalp began to feel itchy.

'Nice thing about living like this is that unwelcome guests don't stay longer than they have to.' Lepping pulled a half-smoked cigarette out of the pile of ash in an overflowing ashtray. He lit it and tossed the match into the hearth, which had become a receptacle for any discarded item that was combustible. 'Let the hearth build up, then I have a fire.'

'I see.' Booth spoke. 'Mr Lepping, your wife disappeared?'

'She walked out on me. Just after our Sara died. That's her.' He pointed to a framed photograph on the mantelpiece. Sara Lepping had in life been a slender-faced woman with short black hair, whose smile revealed perfect teeth. 'Nobody should lose their children. Children shouldn't die before their parents. Not natural.'

'I can sympathise.' Booth spoke softly.

'You have children?'

'Two.'

'You, sir?'

'Just one,' Yellich said. 'A boy.'

'I wanted a son, but when Sara was born I thought, *How could I have wanted a son?* It's true what they say: you can't see past your daughter. She could do no wrong, not in my eyes.'

'Your wife left you?'

'That's what I said. She went to pieces after Sara died. She will have walked into the Humber, just walked in and kept walking. That old river never gives up its dead, you know, just carries you out into the North Sea.'

'Were things well between you and Mrs Lepping?'

'We were married.'

'That's not what I asked.' Pippa Booth held eye contact with Lepping. Lepping took a final long drag on the cigarette and then tossed it into the hearth, where it lay smouldering. 'Sometimes that's enough to start a fire.'

'Answer the question.' Yellich also looked at Lepping. 'Please.'

'You know what married life is like.'

'You haven't always lived here, have you? Our records show you as having an earlier address. Tapping Lane, was it?'

'That's up the posh end of Hedon. That's when I was a farm manager. Had money, a position, status. I was somebody. I could go into pubs, get into a conversation, buy a round of drinks . . .'

'Your neighbours will remember you.'

Lepping shot a glance at Yellich.

'What will they tell us about your marriage?' Booth asked.

'OK.' Lepping poked a meaty finger into the ashtray, as if searching for a cigarette that hadn't been fully smoked. 'Got a cigarette?'

Booth opened her handbag and took out a packet of cigarettes. She handed them to him. 'There's five left. You can have them.'

Lepping, a little wide-eyed at the clearly unexpected act of generosity, nodded his thanks. He took a cigarette and lit it, putting the packet carefully to one side. 'We had fights,' he said.

'Actual fights, or just arguments?'

Lepping paused. 'Well, if she had just done what I told her to do, I wouldn't have had to hit her. You know what marriage is like.'

'Happen often?'

'No . . . no, hardly ever, but it did happen.'

'I see. Did she leave you before?'

'No. She just went to pieces after Sara died, like I said . . . not the same woman. Came back from work one day, she just wasn't home. She was always at home, but that day she wasn't. I told her I wanted her to be at home when I came back each day, like it should be. She was always there with a pot of tea ready for me to drink, then that day she wasn't. No note or anything.' He drew on the cigarette. 'Told the police all this at the time.'

'I read your statement.' Pippa Booth shifted her weight from one leg to the other.

73

'They searched my house, even had dogs sniffing in the garden. They thought I'd murdered her.'

'Did you?'

Lepping shot a glare at Yellich. Lepping may well be a broken man, Yellich thought, but he saw then that there was still a flash of temper and that 'me, me, me' attitude so common among murderers. A senior barrister had once told him that he had been pleading in murder trials all his working life and he had yet to meet a murderer who did not think that the sun shone just for him. And that included the so-called 'crimes of passion'.

'No,' Lepping said at length, 'I did not kill my wife.'

'Or Amanda Dunney?'

Lepping's eyes narrowed. 'Didn't kill her either. That bitch.'

'You threatened to.'

'So would you if she had let your only daughter die in agony. I can't forgive her for that.'

'She disappeared at the same time as your wife.'

'I wondered what happened to her.'

'Really?'

'Yes, really. I couldn't find out her address – probably a good job, probably I would have killed her. She just didn't like Sara being young and pretty. She was – well, the opposite: face like a bat, body like a beached whale. Wasn't Sara's fault. Wasn't our Sara's fault at all. Why bring that bag into this?'

'Because her skull has been discovered.'

Silence. Lepping glanced at Booth, then at Yellich, then at Booth again. 'Her skull? Where's the rest of her?'

'We were hoping you could tell us that, Mr Lepping. And also help us with the identification of the female skeleton that was found with her. It's a skeleton of a woman who was about your wife's age when she was reported missing, by you.'

Lepping shot to his feet. Yellich growled at him, and he sank back into the chair.

'You see the reason for our interest,' Booth offered.

'Well, I didn't do either of them. That's a fact.'

'It is, is it?'

'Aye,' Lepping snarled. 'It is. You'll never prove I did either because I didn't. Simple.'

'Can you remember what you were doing on the day your wife disappeared?'

'A day at the farm. Plenty of people saw me, police checked at the time.'

'But you waited three days before you reported her missing?'

'Thought she'd come home,' Lepping shrugged. 'She would've known she'd get a hiding, thought she was finding the courage to come home and face me.'

'Did that before, did you, when she wasn't at home?'

'Couple of times.'

'How long did she stay away before?'

'One night, two nights . . . I can't remember.'

'So she *did* walk out on you before?'

'So?'

'So . . . only a minute ago you told us she'd never walked out on you.'

Lepping glared at Yellich. 'Stop trying to catch me out.'

'You're tripping yourself up, Mr Lepping. This is a double murder inquiry, and you are a prime suspect.'

'You going to arrest me? I mean, please do, clean sheets and free meals, that has its appeal right now, you know. I mean, look at this, look what a man lives like when there is no woman to look after him. I eat fish and chips every day except Sundays when the chippy is shut, so on Sundays I don't eat. Tomorrow is Sunday – you arrest me, I'll eat on Sunday for the first time in a long time.'

'Not today,' Yellich said, turning to go. Pippa Booth picked up his cue and also turned to the door. 'But we'll likely be back.'

'Don't go too far,' Booth said.

'Where's there for me to go?' Lepping reached for another cigarette.

Walking back to the car, Yellich said, 'Didn't figure you for a smoker.'

'I'm not, but they always come in handy, as you've just seen.'

Miraculously their car had not been vandalised.

'Where would you like to go now?' Booth unlocked the driver's door.

'Tapping Lane. I'd like to talk to his neighbours, see what they recall about him at the time of his wife's disappearance.'

Tapping Lane proved to be located in an altogether different part of Hedon. Here was calm, self-respecting, settled prosperity, neatly tended gardens in which stood well-maintained owner-occupied houses.

'Damn near killed the poor woman.' The frail, white-haired lady leaned heavily on a stout, polished walking stick. Her body was clearly spent, but her alert eyes and speech revealed a mind that retained its youthful sharpness. 'Constantly it was a house of shouts and screams, his shouts, her screams. That house there, across the driveway. You know the address, of course, but twenty feet separates my kitchen from hers. Farm manager! Maybe he could manage a farm but he couldn't manage his own house. But that was him, just had to fight with someone, I bet he was a pig to work for. He could start a brawl in an empty pub. Sydney Lepping . . . I wasn't sorry to see him go.'

'Did his wife leave him?'

'Plenty of times, but she always came back. There's nowt so queer as folk. She'd be wearing dark glasses all the time, and heavy make-up. Didn't take a rocket scientist to work out what she was hiding.' She stood proudly in the doorway of her house.

'Indeed?' Pippa Booth raised her eyebrows. 'Then she disappeared?'

'Aye, now that was a bad time for that family. Poor girl, I watched her grow up . . . she took cancer.'

'So we believe.'

'Wanted to die in her flat in York. I can understand that. Folk who are dying need peace and quiet, but those two wouldn't stop arguing even if their daughter was lying on her deathbed upstairs; they'd argue and fight over the deathbed. That little flat must have been the first bit of peace Sara found.'

'What was he like with Sara?'

'He'd reduce her to tears, right from when she was a small girl, but he never hit her. He didn't have to, he could do all the damage he wanted to do with his tongue, yet in a strange way I think he loved her. I even think he loved his wife. I even think she loved him. Folk are strange.'

'Nowt so queer . . . as you said,' Yellich smiled.

'But he damaged them both, no excuse for that attitude. I'd go so far as to say he murdered his daughter.'

'Murdered her?'

'Aye, well, cancer's a funny business. I lost my man and two of my sisters to it. You get to know about it. There's a "cancer personality", so I've been told: people who are wrapped up in themselves are more prone to the disease than outgoing, volatile people, and after a childhood like she had, she must have been so wrapped up in herself, her mind must have been spinning like a top, but she had no means to express herself. I can see Sara Lepping taking cancer. I can understand it.'

'I think I can too.' Pippa Booth spoke softly.

'You know, I think Mrs Lepping realised the same thing. It was after Sara died, more noise from that house, except for the first time ever I heard her yelling back, giving him as good as she got – *About time too*, I thought. Then it suddenly went quiet, like someone turning off a radio. A few days after that he reported her missing. I told the police at the time. I think they thought he'd done her in. Me personally, I think they were right to think that.'

'You do?'

'Oh, aye. Then he went downhill, took to drinking, heavily. Always was one for his beer, but after that row he was drinking whisky, lost his job, got arrested for the sort of things the village youths get arrested for on a Saturday night. Couldn't keep up the mortgage payments and . . . I still see him in the village from time to time, a mess of a man, and I can't help thinking he deserves what he's become. He brought it on himself. Nice Christian family in that house now. The children bring me hand-made cards each Christmas.'

'What about the people on the other side of the Leppings?'

'They've moved out now. But they weren't at home on that last night when the rowing stopped like a radio being switched off. Only I heard that, and I'll never forget it.'

Driving back to Hull, Pippa Booth said, 'You know, we have enough to arrest him on suspicion. Bet he'd crack under a quiz session. Might even be a relief to him. And it isn't true what he said.'

'About his wife not leaving him before?'

'No, about folk in these part committing suicide by walking into the Humber. They don't, they take sleeping pills, or hang themselves, or slash their wrists, like everybody else. Even the Humber Bridge hasn't become the northern equivalent of Beachy Head, like people thought it would become.'

Yellich glanced out of the passenger window at a group of horses galloping together in a meadow, burning off energy. 'I'd rather leave him where he is; he's right, he's not going anywhere.'

'Your case, your shout.' Pippa Booth paused and then said, 'You know, you have the advantage over me.'

'I do?'

'Yes. You know my Christian name, but I don't know yours.'

Yellich paused. 'Somerled,' he said softly, pronouncing it as 'Sorley', then spelling it for her. 'Somerled Yellich.'

'Somerled! That's a lovely name.'

'I grew to like it. School was a bit of a problem, but I was tall and good at sports, so just one bloody nose and no one else gave me grief over it. Yellich – well, I understand that's a corruption of an east European name, the nearest some harassed customs official could get to pronouncing the original.'

George Hennessey and Louise D'Acre relaxed by the log fire, sipping a brandy; by their body language, their eye contact, they were one, an item. By the approving but discreet looks from the staff, they knew that as their game had worked, as it had been polished over time, this weekend had been a particularly successful play.

'Shall we go up?' Hennessey laid his glass on the low table between their chairs.

'Yes.' D'Acre smiled. 'Let's go up.'

Four

*In which a phone call is received from a gentle-
man in Salop, and DS Yellich is at home to the
gracious reader*

'He's a very likely candidate, boss.' Yellich poised the
coffee cup on his leg and stroked his chin. 'It's all
there really, the motive – he hated, he still hates Dunney
– and his marriage was shaky, shaky and violent. He said
his wife never walked out on him then said she had, so he
lied through his teeth.'

'Enough to arrest him then?' Hennessey leaned back in
his chair, causing it to creak.

'Yes. I was on the verge of it but decided against it.
Pippa Booth, the DS from Humberside – lovely lass –
she said the same thing, enough to arrest him; but as I
said to her, he's not going anywhere. He's totally down
and out, he's nowhere to go, no one to go to. He couldn't
go to ground; if we need to quiz him further, we'll know
where to find him.'

'Very good. Confess I'm rather pleased you didn't
arrest him. Don't know why, but it would seem too . . .
neat, somehow.'

'You think so, sir?'

'Oh yes, I think so. You see, the victims were buried

together in a shallow grave, the head of one, and everything except the head of the other. Somebody clearly
wanted us to assume that we had found the body of
Amanda Dunney, somebody who knew that identification of the dead can be determined by accessing dental
records.'

'Yes . . .'

'So clearly the person who did that was trying to
conceal the identity of the second murder victim. Now,
I can see a man like Lepping battering the life out of
Amanda Dunney, and similarly battering the life out of
his wife, I have no problem with that. What doesn't
ring true with me is that that same impetuous, violent
personality could premeditate not one, but two murders.'

'*Did* he premeditate them, boss?'

'Well, he'd have to make sure both murders coincided.
They only required the one grave didn't they? With the
skull positioned exactly on the shoulders of the other
corpse.'

'Aye, I see what you mean, skipper. Solemn . . . very
solemn.'

'Solemn, as you say, Yellich. But ponder the shallow
grave, often, but not always, associated with premediated
murder, that is in my experience. Burying two victims
in the same grave is speaking loudly to me of very
premeditated murder. There may even be a symbolic or
ritualistic significance to the mixing of body parts, but
whatever, it's very calculating. Do you think Lepping
could be capable of sufficient calculation?'

'Hard to say, boss. He's a fiery temperament, that's
for sure.'

'But does he have sufficient detachment to premeditate
the murder of two women?'

'Pass.' Yellich held up his hand in a gesture of exasperation.

Hennessey smiled. 'All right, impossible question to answer. Put it another way: did Lepping, even when a farm manager and a man with some credibility, did he have the wherewithal to lure Amanda Dunney to her death?'

'Oh.' Yellich's jaw sagged. 'I see what you're getting at, skipper. Well . . . no, I have to say I doubt if he could lure anyone anywhere. His victims would have to be captive, already trapped in some situation.'

'Like marriage?'

'Like marriage,' Yellich conceded. 'So he's not our man.'

'Well, let's not jump to conclusions.' Hennessey smiled. 'Let's not allow ourselves to be over-enthusiastic, but let's not dismiss Mr Lepping too easily. He may still have some explaining to do. Let's just put him to one side for the present. So, what is firm footing in this situation?'

'That the skull belonged to Amanda Dunney.'

'And . . . ?'

'Well, nothing, skipper. That's the long and the short of it.'

'Exactly. What we can assume is that the two skeletons are of people who in life had something or someone in common.'

'Can we?' Yellich asked. 'You see, boss, suppose the victim was the skeleton, and the skull was there to throw us off the scent, the skull of any person, any woman of the right race and age would do, and it just by coincidence happened to be Amanda Dunney. I mean, if that's the case, we're really no further forward.'

'We aren't, are we?' Hennessey sat forwards and rested his elbows on his desk top. 'So what you're saying is that all that hatred surrounding Amanda Dunney at the time of her death was coincidental to the murder of the second victim?'

'It's a possibility, boss.'

'It is, isn't it?'

'You know, what beats me is why the murderer just didn't make a thorough job of disposing of the corpses of his victims. He clearly disposed of one skull and of one body *sans* skull. Not easy.'

'Because folk are queer and twisted and illogical, which makes our job easier. If people thought logically and calmly and gave themselves enough time, their victims would never be found. The underworld do it all the time. If organised crime wants rid of you, you disappear as totally as if you'd been abducted by aliens. I shudder to think how many corpses are in the foundations of the Humber Bridge, or what that motor launch is carrying which sails from the Humber estuary out to the North Sea at dusk, to return an hour or so later. All you need is a weight attached to the body and it'll never be found.'

'It wouldn't, would it?'

'Which brings us back to Lepping. Not a pleasant man, but could he be detached enough to murder not once, but twice, in a short period and then play games with the body parts, switching skulls and everything?'

'You mean there's another shallow grave to be found? Another head and body separated but together?'

'Oh . . . I hope not. But it's a possibility. We're dealing with a real sicko here, Yellich, a real sicko. And that lets Lepping out of the frame, so you were right not to arrest him. He's too volatile. Our man is calm, detached, a man with no outward emotion, so I believe, but I'd like to pick learned brains about this matter. Have you met Camilla Joseph?'

'Don't think so, skipper.'

83

'Delightful woman, really delightful.'

'Can't promise to be of help, Chief Inspector.' Camilla Joseph sat at her desk. Behind her was a large poster advertising Brunei. She was slender, with short hair, dark-skinned but with aquiline facial features. 'And I'm teaching in half an hour.'

'We'll be as brief as we can. Like the poster, haven't seen it before.'

'I went home for Christmas.'

'Ah.' Hennessey then went on to appraise Dr Joseph, forensic psychologist, of the discovery in the shallow grave, of Sydney Lepping, of Amanda Dunney and the hatred she had generated.

'It's clear, as you say, that this man is cold and calculating.' Camilla Joseph pyramided her fingers beneath her chin. 'Any other unsolved murders that you can link to these two?'

'None that we can identify.'

'The detachment that it would take to kill two women, to murder two women, in a short space of time and then have the – the audacity is the only word I can think of – the audacity to mix up the bodies or parts thereof, either as a game, or to evade capture, is a trait of a character which I would consider to be psychopathic.'

'A game?' Yellich asked. He had never met Dr Joseph before, and was taken by her soft-spoken manner and her strong presence.

'It's an old-fashioned term now, and discredited, but once serial killers, for example, were classified as being either organised or disorganised. The organised ones were those who left the bodies of their victims in certain poses, or in public places to maximise the shock value of their discovery; the disorganise ones left their victims where

84

they lay, or attempted to hide the body. The organised serial killers were playing a game as well as murdering people. Strikes me that this fellow, whoever he is, has traits of both. He hides the bodies, yet allows for the possibility of their being discovered, in which case he places the "wrong" head on the skeleton. Intriguing.'

Yellich took his gaze from the view from Dr Joseph's window – the lake, the modern, low-rise university buildings, two female students sharing the same scarf. 'Why – I asked this question of DCI Hennessey – why not just get rid of the bodies?'

'Well, when and if you catch him, you can ask him that, or her, because I have no answer for you. Not for that one. So, the identity of one victim is known, not a popular woman – salvation through suffering indeed! What else do you know about her, her appearance for example?'

'Well, by all accounts her appearance left much to be desired. A very large woman, bat-faced . . .'

'Yes, this could be interesting.'

'What of her lifestyle?'

'Quiet,' Yellich said. 'Lived alone . . . well, alone in a house full of single female lodgers, each with their own room, rather than with a partner.'

'I see.'

'Didn't go out at all after work except for the book club . . . she was a member of a book club, people who meet once a month to discuss a book they've spent the last few weeks reading, then nominate a book to read prior to the next meeting.'

'A reading group?'

'Yes.'

'A book club implies a book-purchasing scheme. So a reading group . . . actual face-to-face contact?'

'Yes.'

'She wasn't a random victim.' Camilla Joseph spoke with calm authority.

'She wasn't?'

'No. Random victims fall into a pattern. Either they are vulnerable and so easy targets – prostitutes, the elderly, for example – or they represent something that the killer wants and hasn't got: they're fulfilled whereas he or she isn't, or they are appealing in terms of their appearance. They attract . . . good-looking young women will attract all kinds of men, and I mean all kinds. The men they fancy and the men they don't. Their looks attract.'

'Amanda Dunney wouldn't have attracted. Is that what you're saying?'

'Yes, in a word, though we mustn't be judgemental. I'm sure Miss Dunney had some good qualities, but by all accounts she had difficulty attracting a partner, and such a woman would not have to fear sexual attack as much as a more attractive woman. So she was murdered for one of two reasons: either there was a motive to murder her, over and above the unnecessary suffering she caused her patients—'

'Why do you say over and above, Dr Joseph?'

'Because any angry relative of one of her patients would be likely to lie in wait for her with a pick-handle, beat her to death, then leg it. They wouldn't go to the trouble of planning the murder and digging a shallow grave.'

'Thank you,' Hennessey smiled. 'That confirms an earlier observation of ours.'

'So, she was killed for a motive, or because she was convenient.'

'Either way, she was known to her attacker.'

'I'd say so.' Camilla Joseph raised her eyebrows. 'But I am of the persuasion that she was killed for her head, which was the right age and sex, to possibly throw you gentlemen off the scent.'

'So someone knew her, someone had her confidence?'

'I would say so.'

'Someone who wanted the other woman dead for a motive.'

'Again, I would say so.'

'Her only social contact was the reading group.'

'And in there you'll find her killer. Look for a male, who would have been in his thirties or forties at the time of her death, possibly a single person, someone whose household is fastidiously kept. A great deal of planning went into this murder, so care and attention to detail are important to this person. He's likely to be strong, well built: Amanda Dunney was not a small woman, and that further points to her knowing her killer. If the killer was slightly built and wanted a skull of a forty-year-old woman, he would have chosen a smaller, more finely made woman whose body was more easily manhandled.'

'That makes sense.' Hennessey nodded and stood up. Yellich did the same. 'Thank you for your time, Dr Joseph.'

'My pleasure. Please feel free to pick my brains any time. I'm sorry I couldn't have been more useful; the pattern left by serial killers is one thing, but a one-off double murder doesn't give a great deal to work with.'

'But enough,' Hennessey smiled, 'to point us in the right direction. You've given us a profile of the offender. That's always useful.'

Walking back across the campus to their car, Hennessey said, 'Back to the reading group, methinks.'

'Seems so, boss, not Dunney's patients or relatives of same after all.'

'I'd like to meet her landlady for myself, and the

organiser of the reading group too. Casting no aspersions about your work, in which I have the utmost confidence, you understand?'

'Of course, sir.'

'Just for my own edification really. The reading group holds the key to this puzzle.'

'I don't think I can tell you anything that I didn't tell the other officer.' Gwen Pedder received George Hennessey in the front room of her house, just as she had received DS Yellich three days earlier.

Hennessey read the room: a woman's house, having a softness of furnishing and decor and a fragrance that only a woman could achieve. The building he thought late Victorian, and best described as 'rambling'. 'Anything else spring to mind about Miss Dunney following DS Yellich's visit?'

'Clearly, as one would expect, a conversation here, a passing glance of her there that I had forgotten, but I haven't recalled anything that would point to the reason for her disappearance. She was obviously troubled just before she disappeared, but I told the other officer that. No callers, no social life that I could detect, and if she had a social life I would have detected it. I make it my business to know about the personal lives of my residents.'

'You do?'

'It isn't interfering, Chief Inspector, it's self-preservation. By allowing people into my house, I leave myself open to being compromised – you would understand that. That is why I insist on professional ladies only, people who have a position to maintain, and a job, a career even, to lose if they break the law. Students, unemployed women, unskilled working women would be more likely to smuggle unthinkable men, or drugs, into my property that would put me in an impossible position as the owner.'

'That's true.' Hennessey nodded in agreement. 'We would charge you as well as your tenant for use of controlled substances. It's the law.'

'Which is an ass sometimes, but it's the law and I therefore keep an eye on my residents. There is a strict no-men rule, and I discourage alcohol on the premises. The regime is a bit convent-like, but that appeals to some women – I think they feel secure. And the all-female house means that within these walls there is an absence of the competitiveness which they have to cope with outside.'

'I can understand that. So, Amanda Dunney: I understand that her only social contacts appear to have been a once-a-month meeting of the reading group she was a member of?'

'So far as I could tell; and her brother, of course. She had occasional contact from him, such as a card at Christmas, that sort of occasional.'

'And she received an invitation to dinner with the reading group. I understand that you remember a handwritten invitation; you mentioned "spiky" handwriting.'

'Did I?' Gwen Pedder raised her eyebrows. 'Yes, I think I did, come to think of it.'

'Can you describe what you meant by "spiky"?'

'Well, spiky . . . pointed.'

'Joined-up letters?'

'No, printed.'

'As if someone was disguising their handwriting, you think?'

'Yes, it could be that sort of writing. In fact it's hard to see anyone writing a letter like that.'

'Big letters, small letters?'

'On the big side, I'd say, took up all the space that was

available . . . very large in fact, sort of shouted at you. I have a grandson who is fascinated by computers. I was talking to him once and he was explaining the good manners of the Internet, and he informs me that capital letters are regarded as shouting if you're in something called a "chat room", or if you are sending e-mail messages. I mention this because the handwriting as I recall it, and as I recall my reaction to it, it did seem like I was being shouted at.'

'That could be interesting. A man or a woman, would you say – by your intuition and as you recall, given the lapse in time?'

'I'd say a man. I would be surprised if it was a woman's printing: the size, the angularity of the lines, no curves . . . Yes, a man's hand, I would say.'

'Now, the last time she left your house . . .'

'Yes, I saw her leave, said goodbye, said I hoped she was going to have a pleasant evening.'

'So she left to attend the dinner, as invited?'

'I presume so . . . she never went out in the evening unless it was to attend the reading-group meetings, and didn't particularly dress up for them. She was always smart in a casual way, but on that occasion she was extra smart, perfumed too. She never wore perfume, a little blusher and some lipstick, but never perfume.'

'But on that occasion she did?'

'Yes.'

'Going to a dinner party?'

'I presume so.'

Hennessey paused. 'From which she didn't return?'

'No. That was the last anybody saw of her.'

'She never had contact from anybody else in the reading group in the interval between the monthly meetings?'

'Not that I was aware of, and I am sure I would have

known about it if there had been contact. I collect the
mail each morning and place it on the table in the hall,
so I know who is receiving letters, and I also answer the
phone and ask who it is that wishes to speak to whom.
Amanda received no personal mail on a frequent basis –
the previously mentioned Christmas card from her brother
was about the extent of her personal mail – and no one
ever phoned her.'

'So she wouldn't be likely to discuss the forthcoming
dinner party with anyone else in the reading group?'

'No . . . she wouldn't.'

'And you don't remember the address at which the
dinner party was being held?'

'I don't. I remember the envelope arriving for her –
she received so few letters, you see – and I did note
a York postmark, but that means nothing, of course.
My grandson with the computer and my daughter live
in Scarborough, and letters posted in Scarborough will
have a York postmark, as I have noticed. So the envelope
could have been posted anywhere in North Yorkshire,
but she clearly valued it: she stuck it to the mirror of her
dressing table.'

'You go into your residents' rooms?'

'Of course.' Gwen Pedder seemed surprised at the
question. 'I have a lady who comes and "does" for
me, and I go round with her. All the girls know that;
it is explained when they look at the available room or
rooms.'

'I see. So she clearly valued the invitation?'

'I had that impression. She had certainly never displayed
one before. My residents are not really partygoers . . . I don't
like good-time girls, and anyway such females would not
want to live in this house. It also came at a difficult time
for her; she was in trouble at work – actually suspended I

91

believe – so it must have been doubly valued.' She paused. 'Why do you ask? You think she was being lured to her death? Oh, my . . .'

George Hennessey stood and thanked Mrs Pedder for her time and her information.

Cynthia Ferguson cocked her head slightly sideways and smiled at the silver-haired man who sat opposite her. In his eyes she saw both wisdom and wounding in equal measure. She also saw a warmth and a kindliness that shone through like a light in the night-time woodland. 'Two visits from the police in nearly as many days, quite remarkable, but I don't think I can add anything to that which I told the other officer, Mr Hennessey.'

'The inquiry is now a little more focused, Mrs Ferguson. Now we are seeking a man who may be described as "fastidious".'

'Fastidious? Hard to please, highly discriminating – that is what I understand by that word. I don't think anybody in our group has ever been fastidious; all are pleased with the group, which is and has always been composed of learned professional persons, but nothing exceptional, not highly learned, not top professional. As in the case of Miss Dunney, in fact: she was a middle-aged nurse and not a very good one at that, or so we found out.

'And was any of the group fastidious about the books we chose?' She gave a slight shrug of the shoulders. 'We chose middle-brow books in the main and nobody objected to any of the choices. So, no, I don't think anyone was ever "fastidious".' There was a pause. Cynthia Ferguson sat in a green dress with a ruby brooch on her left shoulder, legs together and angled to one side, hands clasped on her lap. A cocking of the head, a slight shrug of the shoulders seemed to be the only movement she conceded. At all other times, she was very rigid, as if carved in stone. He wondered if 'supercilious' was the right word. She seemed to him to be a woman who liked playing word games rather than reading. She read the books so that she could score points during the discussion of them, not for the pleasure of the books.

'I don't think any of the group has ever been fastidious. Perhaps you are looking for another word?'

'Neat?' Hennessey shrugged. He thought he had known what Dr Joseph had meant by the word 'fastidious', but now he wished she was there at that moment to clarify.

'Well, there was no dress code, but all arrived smart but casually, so' – Cynthia Ferguson smiled – 'no evening gowns or dinner jackets, but no denims either. "Office smart" is, I believe, the term.'

'Anyone, how shall I say? – excessively neat, who might also have been a little overbearing – pushy, wanting his own way?'

'At the time Amanda disappeared?'

'Yes.'

'You could try Mr Preston.'

'Mr Preston?'

'Yes.'

'That wasn't a name you gave to my sergeant when he called.'

'No it wasn't. You see for some reason he slipped my mind. He was a little loud-mouthed, but like many loud-mouthed people he failed to make a lasting impression. He slipped from my mind, rapidly so, but what does strike me as being of possible interest to the police is that he left the group about the time Amanda disappeared.'

'Did he now?'

'Yes, now. He did.'

'You don't have his address?'

'No, I don't, not after twelve years.'

'I see.' Hennessey paused. 'Could you perhaps describe him.'

'Well, in terms of appearance he was very neatly dressed, exceptionally so. Clean, pressed clothing, highly polished shoes, clean-shaven, not a hair out of place. Tall man, six foot plus, light-coloured hair. Personality: dominant in the group, by voice, not intellect. He wasn't as intelligent as he liked to think. It was easy to win an argument with him, which he didn't like. A man who liked to have his own way. For many years I pitied his wife, and imagined her to be a timid, waif-like creature, then we found out he wasn't married. So he had a servant to attend to his clothes and shoes, or he managed to turn himself out like that unaided, not easy for a man. Not impossible, but not easy. Men, you see, Mr Hennessey, never fail to marvel at the wondrous nature of clothes, how they can be deposited on the floor after being worn and then miraculously appear in the right drawer in a washed-and-ironed, ready-to-wear condition. Astounding. I had three sons, you see.'

Hennessey smiled. He would allow this woman her word games; she accepted people and had a sense of humour.

'But to return to Mr Preston . . . He had the polished manners and confidence of a product of the public-school system. I don't know which one he went to but I don't think it was minor, but probably not one of the Clarendon schools either.'

'The Clarendon schools?'

'Eton, Harrow, Winchester, Charterhouse, et cetera. There are nine of them, all established in the eighteenth century. Four hundred grammar schools were established

at the same time, for the teaching of the classical lan-
guages. It was a great growth in the number of schools,
akin to the establishment of the new universities in the
closing years of the twentieth century.'

'I see. I went to Trafalgar Road School in Greenwich
myself. It was demolished to make way for a block
of flats.'

'Yes. I was at Leeds Girls' Grammar. It's still there.
Or it was, the last time I was in Leeds.' She sat in a
high-backed armchair in a room which Hennessey found
had a solid feel: furniture of old stained wood, wooden
shelves containing hardback books, not a softback book
in sight that Hennessey could see, nor a flimsy trinket
of any kind. Tall windows let in late-afternoon sunlight.
The back garden backed on to fields where a blue tractor,
followed by a flock of birds, ploughed furrows.

'But, Mr Preston?' The smell of artificial fragrance in
the room brought Hennessey's mind back to the matter
in hand.

'Ah, yes . . . not a top-public-school man, nor minor-
public-school either. Middle-ranking school.'

'I see . . . Age?'

'Then, forties, I'd say.'

'What was his Christian name?'

'Miles. Miles Preston.'

'Occupation?'

'Solicitor, I think he said.'

'Easy to trace then?'

'I would have thought so. Why, will he be helping with
your enquiries? I love that phrase.'

'Probably no more than you are, Mrs Ferguson.'

'But you are showing more interest in him than your
younger colleague showed in any of the other members
of the reading group.'

'That is because the focus has narrowed, as I said.'

'Oh yes, fastidious.'

'And because he left the group at about the same time Amanda Dunney disappeared.'

'Of course.'

'You say you believe he was a solicitor?'

'Yes, that's what he told us. We had no reason to disbelieve him, and of course it was a social circle so we didn't ask for references or anything. We just met once a month in this very room for one and a half hours, the first Wednesday of each month, at seven thirty, discussed until nine, had tea and biscuits, and the company had departed by ten. And it still meets. We're reading *Dracula* at the moment.'

'*Dracula*?'

'I told you, it is a middle-brow group, but don't dismiss the novel: it's a sophisticated piece, has many levels.'

'I believe you. I've never been one for fiction. You have a fairly remote house, Mrs Ferguson; I presume the members of the group arrived by car?'

'They did. Amanda came by bus and would be offered a lift back into York, but I don't think she got a lift with the same person on a regular basis. The group members "shared" her. She wasn't popular.'

'I have already formed that impression. Mr Preston's car?'

'A silver BMW with a Ferguson's sticker in the rear window.'

'Ferguson's, the BMW dealership in York?'

'Yes. Same name as me, you see, so I remember it. Any other dealership and I wouldn't have remembered, but it chimed a personal bell.'

'That could be very useful, very useful indeed.'

The front door of the house opened and then shut with

a heavy *clunk*. A dog barked. Mrs Ferguson called out, 'Hello, dear,' then smiled at George Hennessey. 'My husband. He teaches at the university and often finishes early on Mondays.'

The door of the living room opened and a tall, well-dressed man entered. Hennessey stood.

'Darling, this is Chief Inspector Hennessey.'

'Mr Hennessey.' Mr Ferguson extended his hand.

'Good-afternoon, sir.' Hennessey shook Ferguson's hand warmly. Ferguson had a healthy handshake, hand perfectly horizontal. It had once been his experience to have his hand twisted to the horizontal and moved up and down by a particularly aggressive personality. Ferguson's grip was strong, but not vice-like, nor was it the offensive 'wet lettuce' handshake with no grip at all.

'I wondered who the car belonged to.' Ferguson relinquished Hennessey's hand. 'So, the police. No trouble, I hope?'

'Oh, plenty,' Hennessey smiled, 'but not in respect of your household, sir.'

'Mr Hennessey is trying to trace someone who was in our reading group, dear.'

'Oh, I see.'

'Well, I'll leave you at it; I'll take barking mad there for a walk. Nice to have met you, Mr Hennessey.'

'And you, sir.' Hennessey resumed his seat. 'I think I've concluded really, Mrs Ferguson. I think that about wraps it up.'

'You know, there's one thing that did strike me as a little out of the ordinary about Miles Preston: he always paid cash.'

'Cash?'

'Occasionally the reading group went on an outing with a literary theme. We once hired a small motor coach and went to Hawarth for the day, to the Brontë Parsonage and a walk on the moor behind the Parsonage.'

'I see.'

'We did one such outing a year . . . Miles Preston accompanied us on two or three outings, but always paid cash. He paid his share of the coach hire with cash, and on the trip I never saw him use a credit card once, either to buy souvenirs or to obtain money from a cashpoint. Other group members paid by cheque and used credit cards on occasion during the day.'

'But not Miles Preston?'

'No. For some reason he didn't. Odd behaviour for a solicitor.'

'Was rather, wasn't it?' Hennessey paused. 'So it would be fair to say that you never had confirmation of his identity?'

'Yes . . .' Cynthia Ferguson spoke slowly, softly. 'Yes, that would be fair. He made telephone contact with me after reading our notice in Pages Bookshop, and I had no reason to suspect he was using an alias. If, indeed, he was.'

'As you say, but when we cut to the chase, all we know about him was that he was in the group contemporary with Amanda Dunney, left at about the time she disappeared – did he leave by announcement?'

'No, he just stopped coming.'

'I see. And he drove a silver BMW which may have been obtained from Ferguson's. And he had the manners of a public-school-educated man. 'Quite a man of mystery.'

'Wasn't he just? So, I didn't really know who I had in my living room once a month?'

George Hennessey drove the short distance back to York,

to Micklegate Bar Police Station, signed in at the enquiry desk and checked his pigeonhole. Two circulars had been placed in it while he was out of the building. One referred to cost-saving devices: use both sides of a piece of writing paper, make phone calls after 2 p.m. where possible, use second-class postage stamps . . . the same memo was circulated once every six months. The second was an open invitation to the retirement party of DS Sam George. Hennessey knew and liked Sam George and made a mental note to attend the party. He glanced in as he passed Yellich's office: the sergeant was out.

He reached his own office, took the Amanda Dunney file from the cabinet and wrote the recording of his visits to Mrs Ferguson and Mrs Pedder. He glanced at the clock on the wall: four o'clock. The visit to Ferguson's BMW dealership was the next logical step, to attempt to determine the identity of the man who might or might not be named Miles Preston. Unlike the police, Ferguson's would work office hours: no time to get there and ask them to trawl their records of twelve-plus years ago before they shut for the day. That is, if they kept records for that length of time. He drummed his fingers on the desk, and noted the sagging skin and the liver spots on his hands. But they were distinctly more appealing than the alternative, which had been dear Jennifer's lot, and also the lot of—

His phone rang. 'Hennessey.' He spoke calmly.

'Cox speaking.'

'Yes, Mr Cox?' Cox . . . that name rang a bell.

'I phoned earlier. They said you were out. I didn't leave a message. I am Leopold Cox the younger of Salop.'

'Salop?'

'Yes. Now I understand that a body has been found in the York area?'

'Yes.'

'Of a middle-aged woman. It made the national press, you see, just a filler on an inside page. That's how I found out about it.'

'Yes, sir.'

'Well, my wife disappeared in the vicinity of York more than ten years ago now.'

Cox . . . Of course, Hennessey realised: one of the women reported missing at the time of Amanda Dunney disappearance.

'Just alerting you to the fact that it may be my wife. I haven't given up hope of finding her. She would not walk out on us like that.'

'Us?'

'Me and the children. We had four children. All doing very well, confounded the pundits—'

'Sorry?'

'We were once told by a psychologist that if a couple have four children, one will under-achieve. Confounded that fella; all have done well. But it's Marian I'm concerned about. She went looking for her brother.'

'Her brother?'

'Yes. Long time estranged. She went to look him up, to trace him, really.'

'Salop is . . . ?'

'Shropshire to most folk. But I am a medievalist; I prefer the alternative of Salop, evolved from the Middle English "Salopescire", which in turn evolved from the old English "Scrobbesbyrigcir", both infinitely preferable to "Shropshire", but still a delightful county.'

'I don't know it well, I confess.'

'Well, I'm in Bridgnorth.'

'I think I'd like to visit you, Mr Cox. Take a statement. It may be that we have found the body of your wife. The indication is that this female skeleton—'

'Skeleton?'

'Yes, I'm very sorry.'

'That's all right. I was not ready for "skeleton", but after this length of time . . . But in other respects if it *is* her I will be relieved. We can bury her then, you see, say goodbye, put an end to the not knowing.'

'That I fully understand. The skeleton is that of a middle-aged lady who had given birth more than once.'

'Well four times is more than once.'

'And we can date the death to about twelve years ago.'

'Well, it's April now; this coming November will be the thirteenth anniversary of my wife's disappearance. So, how can you pinpoint the date of death?'

'I'd rather not say over the phone, Mr Cox. I do warn you it may be painful news.'

'Very well. You said you wish to see me, take a statement, as they say?'

'Yes, please, as soon as possible.'

'You'll travel here?'

'Yes, sir. When would be convenient?'

'For Marian, any time is convenient. You tell me when you're coming and I'll be here.'

'Well, how about tomorrow?'

'Good. From York you won't get here much before midday. So I'll expect you in the afternoon. Will you be driving?'

'Public transport.'

'Man after my own heart there, it's my proud boast that I've never owned a motor car. Take the train to Wolverhampton, bus or taxi from there. The bus is a hell of a tedious journey, so I usually concede and take the taxi, even though I dislike cars.'

'I'll bear that in mind, sir. Tomorrow, in the early p.m.

Your address is still the same as it was when Mrs Cox disappeared?'

'Yes. Marian's still here, you see, in a sense.'

'I understand that as well, Mr Cox. I'll see you tomorrow.' Hennessey replaced the phone gently and said, 'Oh yes, I understand that only too well.'

Somerled Yellich had left Micklegate Bar Police Station early that day, a privilege of his rank. Often, most often, he was obliged to work long hours, longer that his contract stipulated, but very occasionally he was able to slip away earlier than anticipated. That rainy, sunny, rainy, sunny Monday was one such rare occasion. He drove out of York, across a flat landscape of rich fields to Huntingdon, to a new-build estate of light-coloured brick, to a home standing on a corner of one of the narrow roads in the estate, with a small 'postage-stamp' lawn at the front and an equally small lawn at the rear, and fenced off from the neighbouring houses, as all the estate houses were, with a solid four-foot-high wooden fence, heavily treated with creosote.

As he left his car Jeremy ran down the short path to greet him, colliding with him with such force that Yellich nearly lost his balance. Yellich threw his arm round his son and they walked side by side to the house. Yellich went to the kitchen, where Sarah stood against the work surface; she embraced her husband with powdery arms.

'Jeremy's looking pleased with himself.' Yellich kissed his wife.

'He's been a good boy today, haven't you, Jeremy?'

Jeremy Yellich, aged twelve years, smiled.

'I told him I'd tell you that he'd been good. Helped me in the kitchen, didn't you, Jeremy? All that washing-up you did. And putting away too.'

102

'Good boy, Jeremy.' Yellich hugged his son. 'Shall we do something?'

'Walk.' Jeremy smiled.

'All right, since you've been such a good boy. Wrong time of the year to look for acorns though.'

They walked to a wood and Yellich pointed out different species of tree. They saw a wood pigeon and heard a cuckoo. Mr and Mrs Yellich had been told that, with love, security and stimulation, their only child could achieve the mental age of eleven or twelve by the time he was twenty years of age, and that he could cope with semi-independent living in a staffed hostel, with his own room and access to the kitchen should he wish to prepare his own simple meals.

Later that night, with Jeremy abed, Yellich and his wife sat side by side on the settee sharing a bottle of wine, each telling the other about their day.

Five

In which George Hennessey meets an eccentric

TUESDAY 5 APRIL

Having glanced at the map, George Hennessey had expected to be routed through Sheffield and Birmingham to reach Wolverhampton, so he was not relishing the prospect of the journey. In fact, to his delight, the Northern Spirit service whisked him speedily and efficiently through Leeds and across the rugged 'backbone of England' to Manchester, where he made a good connection with the train for Birmingham. Settling in a forward-facing seat in a sparsely filled but comfortable coach, he enjoyed a journey through Staffordshire. It was a county he did not know and he found the landscape gentle and pleasing to his eye.

At Wolverhampton Station, clearly recently rebuilt, with nothing later than the mid-twentieth century in evidence and with crowded, narrow platforms, Hennessey left the train, exited via the main concourse with the newsagents and stationers to his left and the coffee bar to his right, located the taxi rank and took a cab for the ten-mile journey to Bridgnorth. The taxi driver was clearly a man who didn't travel well and, far from delighting in a drive of an interesting distance, he seemed to resent having to leave Wolverhampton and drove jerkily and aggressively, not speaking at all during the journey. After leaning out of the window and snarling a request for directions, the driver finally located the address given to him by George Hennessey. Hennessey got out of the taxi, having felt disinclined to tip the driver, who drove away with squealing tyres. He glanced at his watch: 1.30. He'd made good time and arrived approximately when he said he would.

The address he'd been given was of a large house, double fronted, with bay windows on both levels. A skylight in the roof spoke of a converted loft – a study, a bedroom perhaps? It was white-painted, brilliantly so in the April sun, and a door painted gloss-black stood at the top of a steeply inclined flight of steps which drove up through a neatly and lovingly tended alpine garden. An ivy plant had been allowed to grow to the left of the door – probably manageable if kept down and well watered, Hennessey thought, otherwise it would draw all the moisture from the mortar and the building would eventually crumble. He had once visited a house where ivy had penetrated the wall and green leaves were seeking sunlight in the living room, beside the television set. As he was looking at this house, the front door opened, and a man in a blue shirt, heavy plus fours and brogues stood in the doorway. He had silver hair, neatly trimmed, and a handlebar moustache.

'Mr Hennessey?' the man called out, over the alpine garden.

'Yes, sir.' Hennessey stepped forward, opened the gate and walked up the steps. 'I was admiring your house.'

'Not a bad pile.' The man held out his hand. 'You should have seen it when we bought it. It *was* a pile then.'

'Really?' Hennessey reached the threshold and took Cox's hand.

'Yes, really. It started life as a house, then became a

warehouse, and a hole had been knocked in the side to allow goods to be craned in and out, and then it lay derelict – no floors, no roof, just a shell.'

'You've done a marvellous job, Mr Cox.' Hennessey turned. About twenty feet below him was the road where he and the taxi driver had parted company with no love lost between them, and beyond the road a green bank with trees and shrubs, and beyond that the river.

'Need the height,' Cox said. 'The Severn is prone to flooding.'

'That's the River Severn?' Yellich turned to Cox.

'That's the Severn all right; gets quite big once it gets past Bristol and Cardiff. Prone to flooding. Lower-lying houses have had a bad time of it in the past, flooded cellars, ruined carpets and furnishings. The water has covered the road in times past and I dare say will cover the road in times to come. So far we have escaped, but only so far; the rise in water level which is predicted by global warming worries me.'

'Worries me too, but I don't think you and I will be around to see the worst of it.'

'No, but my children and grandchildren might. This house represents their future, I wouldn't like to see it washed away. It all started here, you know.'

'Global warming?'

'Yes, in Coalbrookdale, a few miles to the north of here, near Telford. You've heard of Ironbridge?'

'Yes.'

'The world's first iron bridge, bolted together from iron castings like a huge Meccano set. Still stands, open to foot passengers only these days. But that was the take-off of the Industrial Revolution. So global warming started here in this part of the green and pleasant. Strange to think that you can pinpoint the source of the melting ice-caps to a place where the tourist buses still converge. But won't you come in, Mr Hennessey? Let me take your coat. Have you eaten?'

'Sandwich on the train, that'll do me; I don't eat much lunch.' It was a diplomatic untruth. He was in fact quite hungry, but accepting a meal, even a snack, from Mr Cox would have been highly inappropriate. And anyway food wasn't really offered, Hennessey knew that. It was expected of Cox to offer; it was expected of Hennessey to decline. He did however accept the offer of a cup of tea.

He was directed to the living room of the house. It was decorated in late-Victorian or Edwardian style, with heavy, highly polished furnishings of dark wood, green plants in huge vases, but no flowers – that would be too twentieth-century – paintings in wide wooden frames that hung from grey cords attached to a rail three-quarters of the way up the wall. The seat Hennessey chose was an ancient Chesterfield, which smelled of leather and creaked when he sat in it. He avoided the only chair in the room, reasoning that that would belong to the master of the house. Cox entered the room a few moments later carrying a tray on which was a china tea service. He laid the tray on the low table in front of the settee and took the lid off the pot. Steam rose as he put a silver teaspoon inside and stirred the contents.

'Let it infuse for a moment.' Cox replaced the lid with a gentle *click*. In the background a clatter of cutlery was heard from the kitchen. 'Mrs Finney,' Cox explained. 'My housekeeper.'

'Ah.'

'Been with me a long time. Almost as soon as Marian disappeared.' He leaned forward. 'Milk, Mr Hennessey?'

'Please.'

Cox, in his glaringly, outrageously out-of-place blue

shirt, poured a small amount of milk into the bottom of both cups, then poured the tea. 'Help yourself to sugar.' He handed Hennessey a cup and saucer.

'Thank you. I don't take sugar.'

'So few people do, these health-conscious days.' Cox sat back in the chair wisely left vacant by Hennessey. 'So, you have found my dear wife?'

'We may have.'

'Skeletal remains, you said.'

'I'm afraid so, sir.'

'Forgive me, I'm a historian, I work as curator of a museum, I don't wish to encroach on another man's field of expertise, but clothing would decay; metal would not, nor plastic.'

'No, sir.'

'So she was naked?' Cox eyed Hennessey. 'Lack of plastic buttons, the small amount of jewellery she wore, even basic things like bra hooks.'

'Your deduction would have to be correct, Mr Cox. In fact the same observation was made by our forensic pathologist. The skeleton was without any non-biodegradable material in the vicinity.'

'A shallow grave?'

Hennessey nodded.

Cox pointed to his mouth. 'She had gold teeth – I mean, a couple of gold fillings. She was not a lady who liked to spoil herself, and practically was more important to her than fashion, but she once said she liked to show a flash of gold when she talked. So her lower molars, both left and right, had gold fillings.'

'Mr Cox.' Hennessey put the cup and saucer down. 'There is no easy way to tell you this, so I'll just say it. We are having difficulty establishing the identity of the skeleton because we don't have the skull.'

Cox paled and spilled his tea slightly. In the hall a clock loudly chimed the fourteenth hour of the day. Hennessey waited for the chimes to recede before he continued, and when he did he looked down at the brown carpet, avoiding eye contact with Cox. 'We have a skull, but it is not your wife's skull; it was identified as belonging to a . . . another woman of about your wife's age. The skull and the skeleton were in the same shallow grave, which was in a field and was unearthed when the Ouse flooded. You may have seen the photographs on the news?'

'I did; it looked worse than the Severn flood waters.'

'When the water subsided, the becks—'

'Becks?'

'Yorkshire for stream, also "breck" in some parts of the county.'

'I see.'

'Well the . . . streams still ran at full torrent.'

'As they would.'

'One such torrential stream appears to have shifted its course over the years, inching gradually to the left as you look downstream, and unearthed the grave from the side. A farmer noticed the bones protruding from the bank of the stream.'

'I see . . . yes. I have heard that rivers will migrate if they are not encased in rock: the overall course remains the same but they will wander from side to side if they flow over soil. So there's no reason to assume that a stream would not do the same, but on a smaller scale.' Cox seemed to Hennessey to be wandering himself, evading the issue.

'We think the skull was placed with the skeleton in a clumsy attempt to disguise its identity. We identified the owner of the skull from dental records, but that woman was a spinster, had never given birth, whereas the skeleton was that of a woman who had given birth. It exhibited something called "public scarring," which our forensic pathologist advises is caused by not just one, but many births. You and your wife had four children, your said?'

'Yes. All breech deliveries too. I can't see Caesarean section causing the scarring you speak of, but I am no medical man.'

'Nor I, but I think that's a point worth making. All we know is that the skeleton is that of a female in her forties, who had given birth several times, and it is reasonable to assume that she died at the same time as the owner of the skull, being placed in the same grave. The owner of the skull was reported missing a little over twelve years ago; thirteen years this coming December, in fact.'

'Which is when my wife went missing.' Cox placed the cup of tea on the table.

'Your wife's name came up when we checked the national database for missing persons of the age, sex and date, but we didn't connect her at first because her home address was given as – well, this house, but your phone call indicated that she had some connection with the York area.'

'She was looking for her brother.'

'Her brother?' Hennessey leaned backwards, again causing the leather of the Chesterfield to creak. He reached into his jacket pocket for his notebook and took a ballpoint pen from the inside pocket of the garment. 'I'll jot down some notes while we talk, if you don't mind?'

'No, I expect you to. It's the strange thing about television detectives, they never seem to do that.'

'I've noticed.' Hennessey smiled. 'It's quite a glaring omission. We can't retain information like that, we don't have screenwriters doing it for us.' He flicked over the pages until he came to a clean page. 'So it seems to me that we should pick up your wife's trail. It should eventually lead to York.'

'Never been there. Strange admission for a historian to make. Never been to Stonehenge, that's an even stranger admission.'

'Yes . . . Mr Cox.'

'Sorry, I digress.'

'Please tell me as much as you can.'

'Well, my wife's brother was separated from the family at an early age. She remembers him in constant conflict with his parents, and then one day he wasn't in the house any more. He had gone to live in a home for disturbed children. My wife harboured much resentment towards her parents: being the dedicated parent she became, she believes her parents should have hung on – clung on to Andrew no matter what. Andrew Quinlan was his name.'

Hennessey scribbled the name on his notepad.

'Well, as the years went by, Andrew lost contact with his family. The visits to the home got fewer, and my wife said she sensed a feeling of relief in her parents that Andrew was no longer part of the family. That made her feel more angry. She was in her twenties by then. She married, she became a parent, she was fulfilled . . . but there was an emptiness in her life. She always said that when our youngest was sixteen, then she'd make time to find Andrew. So when Colin turned sixteen she said, "Right, that's my duty done, I have a personal quest to address," and she started to search for Andrew Quinlan. First port of call was his residential home.'

'Which was?'

'Mmm . . . I went there with her . . . a bit of moral support. It was called Gyles Place, in Potters Bar, Hertfordshire. Not so far away. My wife came from Stevenage, so Potters Bar was relatively close. And it was a specialist unit, it specialised in accommodating highly intelligent children who had emotional difficulties that prevented them from functioning in the mainstream of life. Not one of the horror-story homes you read about from time to time.'

'I see.'

'I was not unimpressed with the staff, they seemed very enthusiastic, but the tension in the building was palpable. When we visited, one girl had a temper tantrum. I can still hear the screams, you'd think she was being murdered. The principal was clearly embarrassed. As we heard staff running to the scene, he explained that another child had probably used one of her crayons or some such, but that same girl was sixteen years of age and had an IQ that could take her to Oxford or Cambridge. It was a unit for that sort of child.

'But Marian was convinced that her brother's behaviour was caused by his being rejected by his parents; a "created crisis", I think she once called it. With a different parental approach, Andrew wouldn't have been a problem, so Marian believed. But to continue . . . Well, no member of staff actually recalled Andrew – he had left Gyles Place by then and all records had been centralised – but the principal did promise to have the archives searched to see if they had records of what had happened to young Andrew Quinlan.'

'And?'

'And, he made it to university.'

'Don't tell me, York University.'

'Leeds. Near enough. So by then Marian had the bit in her teeth and travelled to the north country, alone this time. That was the last I saw of her. She stayed in an inexpensive hotel and phoned me to say she had contacted one of his old tutors. That was fortunate. Twenty years on, you see, the tutor had to be middle-aged by then, minimum.'

'Didn't mention his name?'

'She did not, but she was shown a photograph. The tutor dug out a year-group photograph and showed it to her, and Marian described a handsome, fair-haired young man . . . she was thrilled, really thrilled. Two days later she said she had found out where her brother lived and that she was going to call on him, surprise him. "Be the best Christmas present we could both wish for" were effectively her last words to me.'

'You didn't know the faculty at Leeds University?'

'I'm sorry. She never said.' Cox paused.

'You look worried, Mr Cox.'

'I am. I am misleading you.'

Hennessey raised an eyebrow.

'I have missed out a step. Thirteen years . . .'

'It's all right, take your time.'

'I remember, now, that Andrew had a gap year between leaving Gyles Place and going to university. What he did I don't know, where he went I don't know, but he kept in touch with Gyles Place – nearest thing he had to a family, you see – and told them he was off to university.

'Then Marian went to Leeds. I just assumed it was Leeds University that he had gone to, but there are a lot of universities round there, aren't there?'

'And neither she nor the staff at Gyles Place ever specifically mentioned Leeds University?'

'No.'

Hennessey paused. 'We'll have to pick up the trail at Gyles Place,' he said, more to himself than to Cox. 'Find out what or who brought Mrs Cox to Leeds.' Again he paused. 'There is still no certainty that the skeleton is that of Mrs Cox.'

'It is. It will be, my waters say so.'

Hennessey nodded; he too knew of his 'waters'. 'Mrs

Cox didn't have any distinguishing feature about her skeleton? No malformation, no old fractures?'

'Marian was perfectly formed, chief inspector. A lovely woman, greatly missed, even now. I don't know how big a hole she filled when she died, but the hole she has left behind her is immense.' Hennessey smiled. He knew that notion as well. 'And no, she had no old fractures, nothing of that sort.'

Hennessey stood, and thanked Cox for his time and information.

Being under no time pressure to return to York, Hennessey strolled into Bridgnorth. He discovered a pleasant market town, steeped in history. He found the terminus of the Severn Valley Steam Railway; he found an abundance of eating places and took a late lunch in one such. It was obviously a place to bring Louise D'Acre on one of their rare weekends off together: antiques shops for her and steam locomotives for him.

By contrast with the previous driver, the man who drove Hennessey to Wolverhampton was jocular and talkative – annoyingly so. Hennessey made an excellent connection at Manchester Piccadilly, was in York by seven and home to an excited Oscar at eight.

WEDNESDAY 6 APRIL

The rain had lifted. Wednesday dawned bright, clear and sunny, chilly outside, especially in the wind, but visibility was perfect. Hennessey drove into York and to the police station, parking his car beside Yellich's. Inside the building he saw Yellich standing by the table in the corner of his office, pouring boiling water into a coffee mug.

'Any joy yesterday?' he asked.

'No, boss. Well . . . I'll tell you. Coffee?'

114

'Yes, I'll have a mug, thanks.' Hennessey stepped into Yellich's office.

'Well, I phoned the BMW dealership like you asked. They have computerised their records going back twenty years.'

'And?'

'No customer by the name of Preston had purchased a vehicle from them since their records began until the time of Amanda Dunney's disappearance.' He handed Hennessey a mug of steaming coffee.

Hennessey took the mug, laid it on Yellich's desk and turned it round so that he could pick it up by the handle. 'That tells us . . . well, what does it tell us?'

'That Mr Preston's car was second-hand. That's what I assumed. The first owner bought it from the dealership, and sold it leaving the dealer's sticker in the rear window. My old Ford is second-hand but the dealer's sticker is still in the rear window. I'm not bothered whether it's there or not, but it occurred to me that some folk might deliberately leave the sticker in the window to give the impression that they had bought the car new.'

'All right, if it tells us that. Possibly. It possibly also tells us that Preston is an assumed name. People wouldn't have to prove their identity when joining the reading group, unlike applying for a job, for example.'

'Wouldn't, would they, boss?' Yellich nodded. 'If that's true, it points a suspicious finger at Preston.'

'Who, of the reading group, is remembered as being obsessively neat, the likely profile of the murderer suggested by Dr Joseph. Do you think a neat person, a fastidious person, would be careful with his car?'

'I would think so, boss.'

'So would I. So why don't you phone the dealership back? What was their name?'

'Ferguson's.'

'Of course, same as the organiser of the reading group. Yes, phone them, describe Miles Preston, well built, muscular, blond hair, always well dressed, ex-public-school mannerisms.'

'Will do, boss.'

'You know, if Miles Preston was an assumed name used in the reading group, it would explain why he always paid for his outings in cash.'

'Avoided using a cheque?'

'Exactly. I mean a man with a BMW would chip in his fifteen-quid fee with a cheque.'

'You'd think so, boss, you'd think so. Yes. I'll get right on it.'

Hennessey carried the mug of coffee to his office and sat at his desk. He glanced out of his window at the medieval walls of the ancient city, at that moment gleaming in the morning sunlight. They were deserted, the stretch that he could see, but later, even on cold, windy days in April, the walls would be carrying tourists aplenty, and, thought Hennessey as he turned from the window and picked up his telephone, not a few locals too. He pressed a 9 for an outside line, then dialled Directory Enquiries. He asked for the number of Gyles Place Children's Home, Potters Bar, Herts. There was a moment's pause; the operator, who sounded to Hennessey to be already tired at 8.45 a.m., said that there was a listing for Gyles Place Children's Centre, and she wondered if that could be it. Hennessey asked for the number, saying he would soon find out. The line clicked and a mechanical-sounding voice dictated the number slowly enough for Hennessey to write it down without needing to listen to the repeat.

'We don't like the term "children's home".' The voice on the other end of the line was warm, confident. 'It has old-fashioned connotations. We're much more than custodians of children. It's a highly specialist unit, we have referrals from all over the country.'

'You are the senior man, Mr . . . ?'

'Pym. Yes, I am the principal, or the officer in charge, either title is acceptable. And you are the police, from York?'

'Yes. DCI Hennessey. This is a bit of a long shot, but many years ago a boy called Quinlan, Andrew Quinlan, was admitted to your custody.'

'Care. He would have been admitted to our "care."'

'Sorry.'

'Quinlan. That's not a name I recall, but I've only been here for five years.'

'This was a lot longer ago than that.' Hennessey allowed his smile to be heard down the phone. 'We are talking perhaps forty years.'

'Forty! Blimey. Gyles Placc has been open as a children's centre for that length of time, but nobody here has been here for more than . . . well, ten years at the most. There is always a fast turnover of staff in children's homes, even in agencies like ours with highly motivated staff. Pay's poor for junior staff and the stress levels are high. Stress is contagious, you see: one highly stressed individual can transmit his or her stress to another and cause that other to become stressed, and the junior staff work more closely with the children, all of whom are highly disturbed, but also highly intelligent, so they pick up the most stress.'

'I didn't think there would be anybody's brains to pick, but two things occurred to me. Firstly, you may have contact with retired staff members who could reach back that far in their memory.'

'Not offhand, but I'll help all I can.'

117

'The second possibility is accessing the record of Andrew Quinlan. I understand that is possible?'

'His file will be held in the archives. We are a charity, not a local authority. The head office is in Potters Bar, whereas we are just outside the town. I can give you their number.'

'Many thanks.'

Hennessey phoned the number given by Pym.

'I'll have to put you through to Mr Standish.' The telephonist had, in Hennessey's view, an annoying speaking voice, slow, as if dim-witted. Not the right person for a job as a telephonist. The line clicked; there was a a long silence, then a snappy, aggressive voice said, 'Standish.'

Hennessey paused. He used this technique to slow telephone conversations. 'Yes . . . police here, York City.'

'Yes!'

Hennessey paused again. 'I'm making an enquiry in respect of a boy who passed through the care of Gyles Place some forty years ago.'

'Yes, we will have a record of him. Name?'

'Quinlan. Andrew.'

'Right. Give me your number and I'll phone you back.'

Hennessey did so and the phone was slammed down. Hennessey said, 'Thank you very much,' knowingly into a dead line and replaced his own receiver, gently. He waited, glancing out of the window of his office. Tourists, as he had anticipated, now trailed over the walls. He looked around his office, at the grey Home Office-issue filing cabinet, at the Police Mutual calendar, at the small potted plant that needed watering. He made a mug of coffee, drank it as he waited, watered the plant, caught up on a little paperwork.

Then his phone rang.

'Hennessey,' he said as he picked it up.

'Standish. Sorry for the delay in getting back to you.'

Hennessey glanced at his wristwatch. 'Only twenty-five minutes.'

'I was accessing the file, or one of the secretaries was.'

'Thank you.'

'So, young Quinlan.'

'Young Andrew Quinlan.'

'Yes, referred to us because his parents couldn't cope with his aggressive and disruptive behaviour, smashing the family home up . . . Had a period of assessment in another home, set all the lights flashing at the intelligence test so they referred him to Gyles Place.' There was a pause; Standish was clearly reading the file. 'There are the daily recordings by the staff . . . records of parental visits, not many of them, poor lad . . . letters from his sister – he was encouraged to reply, but seemed reluctant. It's quite a hefty file, Mr Hennessey. Is there something specific you wanted to know?'

'Well, specifically where did he go when he left Gyles Place?'

'Moment . . .' Standish turned what sounded like a handful of pages. 'He was eighteen when he left us. That's quite old in normal circumstances, but not so old for Gyles Place. It would mean he was studying, doing pre-university qualifications – clearly one of the successes, calmed down enough to address long-term study. He is recorded as leaving to do voluntary service in the north of England, a 'gap year' as I believe it's called. That was thirty years ago. These old files . . . reading them is like getting into a time machine, the forms they used, but they served just as well as the forms we use today. You know that observation about change bringing an illusion of progress but really creating confusion? It is so true.'

'Yes . . . does it say where he went? Exactly?'

'Not in the file, just the address of the charitable organisation to which he gave his time in return for board and keep and a bit of pocket money. Wait a minute, I'll look at the letters . . . private correspondence . . .' There was another pause on the line. Hennessey heard the rustling of paper, heard a tap on the door and Standish say, 'Come back in ten minutes will you?', then a further silence, broken by Standish saying, '181 Victoria Road, Leeds 6, family by the name of Wall.'

'Wall?'

'That's it, as in "within these four walls". Young Quinlan wrote a series of letters to a fellow called Tom Silva, obviously a member of staff that he had bonded with. Quinlan thought it was a personal exchange but Silva, probably sensibly, filed them. There's six in all, short notes really, ends with Quinlan wishing Silva well in his new job and asking for his new address.'

'Any indication of Andrew Quinlan's appearance?'

'No . . . I'm looking at the front of the file . . . no photograph . . . Oh, a report here beginning with describing him as being of "Caucasian extraction". Today we'd say "white European". Average build, dark hair, no physical infirmity, no particular distinguishing features like birthmarks or anything of that sort. So he left us, seeming to be alone in the world, and went to live in Leeds. Where then we have no idea. Some start to life.'

'Wasn't it just?' Hennessey thanked Standish for his help and replaced the telephone receiver, again quite gently, though he had noted that Standish's bullish manner had mellowed a little during the conversation. He recorded the information in the growing file on the headless skeleton – at that moment still identified by file number, but which, Hennessey was convinced, would become the file on Marian Cox, née Quinlan – and cross-referred it to the file on Amanda Dunney. That done, and the file placed neatly in the filing cabinet, Hennessey left his office and walked to the end of the corridor, to the office of Commander Sharkey.

'Come in, George.' Sharkey allowed himself a brief smile as Hennessey stood on the threshold of his office.

'Just want to apprise you, sir.' Hennessey walked into Sharkey's office.

'Good, take a pew. The double murder, I take it?'

'Yes, sir.'

Sharkey was a young man, young to hold the rank of commander. A framed photograph on the wall behind him of a younger Sharkey in the uniform of an officer in the Royal Hong Kong Police, and a second photograph, showing an even younger Sharkey in the uniform of a junior officer in the British Army, told the life of the man and his route to his present position. He was also small for a police officer, a man who showed that if the selection board think a man is made of the right stuff the lack of an inch or two in stature can be overlooked. Sharkey was neatly turned out. Now here, thought Hennessey, here was a man he'd describe as 'fastidious'; groomed to perfection, not a hair out of place, perfectly ironed shirt, neat pinstriped suit, shoes hidden beneath his desk but doubtless polished to a mirror-like sheen. All on his desk was clearly where it should be. Hennessey doubted that he could spend much time in the company of Commander Sharkey, and felt for his wife and children, who seemed to be standing to attention in the photograph on his desk.

Hennessey adjusted his position in the chair. 'We are making progress. I think the skeleton, the bit without a head, will transpire to be that of Mrs Marian Cox, who came north from Shropshire about twelve years ago to search for her estranged brother. Exactly what was the link between her and Dunney we don't know, but Dunney's only social outlet was a reading group. Having your head chopped off and placed in a shallow grave is not the work of stranger murder. It speaks of acquaintance murder and motive.'

'It does, doesn't it?'

'Dr Joseph at the university, a forensic psychologist, has stuck her neck out for us and suggested that the murderer might be . . . well, she used the word "fastidious", in his lifestyle and appearance.'

'Fastidious, like me, George?' Sharkey smiled again, briefly.

'Just fastidious. It is Dr Joseph's contention that severing the skull from the skeleton and placing it with the skeleton of another murdered woman had two purposes.'

'To throw us off the scent being one?'

'Yes, sir. And the other for shock value, should the grave be discovered. Apparently that sort of "shock value" at the point of discovery is the hallmark of what I believe were once called "organised serial killers", all of whom prove upon arrest to lead very neat, organised—'

'And fastidious lives.'

'Apparently so, yes, sir. The so-called "disorganised" serial killers just leave their victims where they fall and run off into the night. And of Amanda Dunney's social contacts, one man who was a member of the reading group was of exceptionally neat appearance.'

'You believe he's the link between Amanda Dunney and Marian Cox?'

'I think so, commander.'

'Your next move?'

'Well, I asked DS Yellich to visit a BMW dealership – the neatly dressed man drove a BMW – and I thought

I'd follow Marian Cox's trail in search of her brother. See where that leads. Already traced him to an address in Leeds, which is a lot closer to home than his previous address, in Hertfordshire.'

'I'll say.' Sharkey paused. 'About other matters, George . . .'

'Yes, sir?' Hennessey said, though he knew what was coming and that his answers would be 'no' and 'no'.

'Two things, George.' Sharkey paused. 'I know that I have asked you this before, and on more than one occasion to boot, but it is a concern of mine; I saw enough of it in Hong Kong.'

'There is no corruption at Micklegate Bar Police Station, sir. I would know. I have been a copper pretty well all my working life, straight into the Navy for my National Service, then joined the police. Swapped one blue uniform for another. I have in the past known a bent copper or two, but there's nothing to worry about in this nick.'

'Relieved to hear it. Even though you can't know for certain – no one can – but you, with your finger on the pulse of this station, if anyone knows it would be you. Didn't have to do anything for it, you know, just opened my desk drawer each Monday and there would be a brown envelope there, a small number of large-denomination notes. And when I say large, I mean large. I was given more money each week than my monthly pay. I earned it by not asking questions. I was occasionally told by my sergeant not to send a patrol into a certain district at a certain time, or he'd tell me to send patrols into a particular district at a particular time, so as to ensure that another district was without a police presence. On other occasions he'd tell me not to turn up for duty. He'd tell me to spend the evening at the yacht club, or stay at home; he said he'd cover for me, which he did. I never knew what was happening but heroin would be at the bottom of it, without a doubt. I just had to do what I was told by the man who addressed me as "sir", and each Monday morning there it would be, an envelope full of money. I wasn't there very long, George: I left because of the corruption. If I hadn't taken the money I would have been found floating in the harbour among the blue dolphins, with my throat slit.'

'Hobson's choice, if you ask me, sir . . . and you did leave because of the corruption.'

'Yes, but I took it. It's still with me, that money. It's a long time ago now but when I returned to England I used it to buy my first house. As I, as we, have moved up the housing ladder, that money has moved up with us. It's still in our bricks and mortar. My children will inherit it. If I donate the corresponding amount in today's terms to a charity, would that solve the problem? Would I be giving tainted money to charity? The tainted money is in the house, in my finances, like a dormant virus. I should never have gone to Hong Kong, never. I keep that photograph of myself because it's part of my history and I want to be reminded of it, of my time there. If you forget your past, you are doomed to relive it.'

'Good point, sir.'

'It's not original. Santayana said it; the exact quote, I think, is "Those who do not remember the past are condemned to relive it."'

'Santayana, sir? I don't know that name.'

'George Santayana, a Spaniard, born mid to late nine-teenth century, taught at Harvard.'

'I see.'

'A man of wisdom.'

'Seems so.'

'But back on track, George: you will let me know of anything like that, even the slightest suspicion?'

'I will, sir.'

'Good. Now, the other point. George, I cast no critical comment on your work, but are things all right with you?'

'Yes, sir, I feel on top of things.'

'You'll be making retirement plans?'

'Yes, sir. I plan to travel about Great Britain. There are many parts of this right little, tight little island that I haven't visited. I plan to travel widely but within these shores, and to stay awhile in each place – not an "If it's Tuesday this must be Ipswich" sort of holiday, but a getting to know the locality as much as I can. When you're alone in a strange town and have a night to kill, the best form of entertainment is to visit five or six pubs, have a pint in each and just keep your eyes and ears open; you really get a feel of the local community.'

'I'll remember that. How do you feel when you drive to work each morning? Confident? Happy?'

'Well, yes . . . unless something is troubling me.'

'This morning?'

'Confident, content, planning the day, knew I had a phone call to make, wanted to apprise you, sir . . . normal thoughts about the day ahead.'

'I want you to enjoy your retirement, George. Only a few years to go. I have also told you about one of my teachers, from my schooldays, Johnny Taighe . . .'

'I think you have, sir.'

'Smoked like a chimney, drank like a fish – his red nose said so – carried too much weight. He was close to retirement, should have been allowed to soft-pedal, but they pressured him, gave him a job he wasn't up to. No energy left, he was burnt out, and they piled on the pressure; he keeled with a massive coronary. All the warning signs were there – the smoking, the drinking, the weight, that false good humour that says nervousness,

125

unhappiness – and his colleagues missed them all. It won't happen to any of my staff.'

'Well, I'm not overweight, sir, I no longer smoke, I drink minimally and feel sufficiently energetic. I don't want to police a desk, but thanks for the concern.'

'All right, but no comment was intended about your performance. I have no complaint about it.'

'Thank you, sir. Will that be all?'

'Yes, thanks, George. Thank you.'

It was midday. Hennessey signed out and walked the walls to Lendal Bridge, then to the Old Starre Inn in Stonegate, for a pub lunch of passing satisfaction. He ate it in a seat in the corner, beneath a framed print of an old map of 'Yorkshyrre', 'with ye famous and Fayre citie York defcribed'.

'Well, I wasn't here then, Mr Yellich.' The man was sharply dressed, clean-shaven, with a gentle whiff of aftershave. His office was neat, functional, airy and well lit; a large calendar beneath a photograph of an early model of a BMW hung on the wall. 'Can't think who could help you. Ah, wait! Tom Dyett might.' The man picked up his phone and dialled a two-figure number. 'Julie,' he said when his call was answered, 'is Tom Dyett in at the moment? Thanks.' He replaced the phone. 'Well, he's working at the moment. If he can't help you, you've drawn a blank. Possibly. Tom is the only one who is still with us who was here twelve years ago. I'll take you to him.'

Yellich was escorted to the workshop of the dealership, where tools clanged and buzzed, where mechanics in light blue overalls with *Ferguson* in German racing silver printed on the back leaned over open bonnets, or peered up at the underneath of cars on the ramps.

Tom Dyett was a short, stocky, middle-aged man who

wore spectacles. He held up a dirty, oil-caked palm and said, 'Won't shake hands.'

'I'll leave you two, then.' The salesman turned and walked away.

'Let's go outside.' Tom Dyett nodded to the open doorway which led to the car park at the rear of the dealership.

'Wouldn't have his job.' Dyett nodded over his shoulder. 'Young Ferguson, or "Ferguson the youth" as he's known on the shop floor. It was his father that started this outfit. Look at all this metal.' Dyett looked out over the car park. 'There must be sixty cars here, all wanting owners. What this represents in money I can't imagine. The cheapest must be priced about the same as your annual salary, and don't ask about the most expensive. All he's got to do is sell them. They haven't sold a car for three weeks. Me, I don't run a car, more trouble than they're worth. I can take 'em apart and put 'em back together, but I travel by bus. It's good to get outside.' He breathed deeply. 'So, how can I help you?'

'We're trying to trace a man.' Yellich looked over the roofs of the cars to the grassy bank that surrounded the car park, the high metal fence atop the bank, the blue sky above. 'He was known to drive a BMW with a Ferguson's sticker in the rear window. Doesn't mean he's a customer, of course, could have bought the motor second-hand, but just in case he was a customer, then he'd be in his forties, large, well built, light-coloured hair, well dressed. Ring any bells?'

'Bit pukka? Posh accent?'

'Yes.' Yellich allowed a note of hope to enter his voice.

'Well, this is serious-money territory, so a lot of our customers are pukka, but the blond hair, that sounds like Mr Quinlan.'

'Quinlan?'

'Yes, Mr Andrew Quinlan. He's an accountant – was then, hasn't been back for a few years now, probably changed his make of car, Rolls-Royce by now, probably. But he wasn't toffee-nosed like some of our customers. He'd chat to you, pass the time of day . . . helped me financially.'

'Loaned money?'

'No . . . advice. Ferguson's don't give pensions, they can't, so I asked Mr Quinlan for advice. He told me to avoid private pensions because you pay more in than you get out. He suggested I borrow some money and buy a terraced house to let to students, told me where in the city to buy the house, told me the name of a reputable finance house to borrow from. I've got six houses now. The rental is more than the payments and I'll have the loans paid off before I retire, then the rent is all profit, after tax, and maintenance to the buildings. A very nice pension, thank you very much. I owe that to Mr Quinlan.'

'Andrew Quinlan,' Yellich repeated, then added, 'Thank you, thank you very much, Mr Dyett.'

'Hope he's not in trouble.'

'I don't know myself, yet.'

'Wouldn't want anything bad to happen to him. Like I said, I'm financially safe because of him. 'Well, if you could give him my regards.'

'Yes, if I can.'

Yellich returned to the airy, well-lit office of 'Ferguson the youth' and asked if he could access the computerised files for one Andrew Quinlan. The address flashed upon the screen: Cuckoo's Nest, East Riding Way, Nether Poppleton.

'Pukka all right,' said Yellich, noting the address in his book. 'Very pukka.'

Six

*In which the chief inspector visits Leeds and is later
at home to the gentle reader*

Hennessey took the train to Leeds. He had lived
with a long-term, near-lifelong dislike of motor
transport, save perhaps buses, and had always far, far
preferred travel by train. For the second time in the space
of twenty-four hours he travelled by Northern Spirit from
York Station, although on this occasion he terminated his
journey at Leeds, and, being unfamiliar with the city, he
took a taxi to Victoria Road.

Victoria Road, he found, was a long, straight, gently inclined thoroughfare lined with spacious-looking
nineteenth-century houses in terraces. There were small
shops and launderettes and Indian restaurants at inter-
vals amid the red-brick terraces. A group of youthful-
looking people stood at a bus shelter: university students,
Hennessey guessed. Number 181 was at the bottom end
of the road, close to the intersection with a winding main
road, generously lined with mature trees.

He walked up the short flight of steps to the green-
painted door on to which the numbers '1', '8' and '1' had
been screwed in individual brass numerals. He pressed the
doorbell but heard no sound from within, so he tapped the

129

small metal knocker. He was about to knock again when the door opened slowly to reveal a frail, elderly woman and a dark, cavernous hallway behind her.

'Mrs Wall?'

'Yes, I am Mrs Wall.' The woman spoke clearly, strongly. Her body may well have succumbed to age but Hennessey was grateful to find that her mind was still youthful and strong.

'I am Detective Chief Inspector Hennessey of the York Police.' He showed his ID. 'I wonder if I can ask you some questions, Mrs Wall?'

'You may. Would you like to come in? Would you care for some tea after your journey?'

'Thank you.'

Mrs Wall turned round slowly and walked back down the corridor. 'Do come in,' she said with her back to Hennessey, 'and please close the door behind you. This is Headingley, twenty-four-hour burglary threat.'

Hennessey stepped over the threshold of the old house, sweeping off his hat as he did so. The door was large and heavy, but swung easily on its hinges and closed with a satisfyingly loud *click* of the barrel lock.

'Thank you,' said Mrs Wall in response to the sound.

She led Hennessey into a large, spacious room. A young woman in an apron looked curiously at him as he entered the room.

'I know what you're going to say, but he's a policeman.'

The younger woman smiled at Hennessey, then turned to Mrs Wall and said, 'Even so, I wish you'd let me answer the door.' She turned to Hennessey again and said, 'One day she'll answer the door to the wrong person; they just barge in, you know.'

'You worry too much, my child.' Mrs Wall turned,

sank with some effort into an upholstered upright chair, and tipped the walking stick beside it. 'Good day. Today's a good day. Didn't need my stout little crook-handled friend today. Mr, er . . . ?'

'Hennessey.'

'Mr Hennessey has come from York. Do you think he could have a cup of tea, girl?'

'Of course.' The 'child' or 'girl' in question, who Hennessey guessed was in her forties, and with engagement and wedding rings upon the appropriate finger, smiled and walked out of the room.

'Don't know what I'd do without her,' Mrs Wall said as the housekeeper left the room. 'Do sit down, please, Mr Hennessey.' Hennessey sat in an armchair opposite Mrs Wall, whose manner was formal and reserved, but whose eyes were sincere and warm. 'Now, young man, what can I do for you?' She wasn't a Yorkshirewoman; she was clearly a long-term resident of the county but her accent betrayed her an incomer. Hennessey thought he detected a trace of Norfolk in her speaking voice, perhaps Suffolk, but definitely East Anglia. 'Not in any trouble, I hope?'

'Not at all, Mrs Wall. It's actually in connection with a young man, a name from your past you may remember. Andrew Quinlan.'

'Andrew!' Mrs Wall smiled. 'Well, you are picking over an old woman's memory. Andrew lived with us for a year, in this house; he had the attic bedroom. Lovely young man, seemed to appreciate being a part of a family; he had grown up in a children's home.'

'So I believe.'

'It's going back to when Tom was with us.'

'Tom?'

'My youngest. He was born without eyesight or hearing

and because he was deaf his speech was limited. You can teach a dumb person to speak if they have sight, because they can see words being mouthed; by mimicking the mouthing action they can learn to enunciate. But Tom had neither sight nor hearing, and although he could make sounds he never could learn to speak. Andrew was placed with us to be Tom's eyes and ears for a twelve-month period. Andrew came when he was eighteen and Tom was just twelve. He is in an institution now . . . I grew too frail . . .'

'I understand.'

'It's thirty years, I should think it's about thirty years since Andrew came to live with us. I'm eighty-three, Tom is forty-two – he was a late baby; that'll mean Andrew Quinlan is now in his fifties.'

The housekeeper entered the room carrying a tray of tea and laid it on the coffee table, which she then picked up and placed just in front of Hennessey. 'I brought a second cup in case you'd like one, Mrs Wall.'

'I won't: too soon after lunch.'

'Shall I pour for you, sir?' the housekeeper asked of Hennessey. Hennessey smiled his thanks and said he'd manage. The housekeeper left the room, padding silently on soft-soled shoes, shutting the door behind her.

'His sister came here too, you know. Never knew he had a sister till she presented herself at my door, about ten years ago, possibly a little more than ten years ago.'

'I'm following the same trail.' Hennessey poured the tea into a china cup decorated with delicately painted yellow flowers.

'It's bad, it's sad, it's mad when blood relatives become estranged.' Mrs Wall winced momentarily. 'I have other children, two sons and a daughter. I insist that they visit Tom as often as they can, and they do. Tom . . . he has a sense of touch and also of smell, and he uses those to recognise people. He feels your face and takes your scent and can express joy and sorrow, he can be communicated with. He could find his way all over this house and remember where he had left his possessions.

'He and Andrew bonded with each other. They would go out for afternoons up to Golden Acre Park, or Woodhouse Moor, which, if you don't know Leeds, is a cultivated park despite its name. And they would hold hands and run on the grass. I went with them when I could, saw how much Tom enjoyed that. That was Andrew's idea, that's the sort of young man he was. You see, Mr Hennessey, he realised how frustrated Tom was, intellectually as well as physically. Andrew seemed to "see" Tom. He saw that he had a brain that had no outlet, no expression. He realised that a twelve-year-old boy shouldn't be cooped up in his body. Other helpers before Andrew would take Tom for a walk, but it was Andrew who actually taught him to run, and to have the confidence to run. Andrew Quinlan was a very good young man.'

'Where did he go when he left your home?'

'He stayed in Leeds. He seemed to take to this area, Headingley, on the borders of Burley Park. Leeds 6 is where all the students live. Most of the houses in Victoria Road are student lets, and the area has a certain "buzz", a "vibrancy". I think Andrew picked up on it, and decided to stay. He moved out of our house, but retained contact with us. Sometimes he slipped and referred to this house as "home". He was clearly very socially isolated, but also clearly he moved on in life, and after he graduated we had no further contact with him.'

'Do you have his last address?'

'I don't. It would only have been a damp and miserable

bedsit. His sister asked the same question, and back then I thought I might have had it, but I've had a clear-out since then. I remember I advised her to go to the university. He studied accountancy. I believe they keep some kind of record of their students' forwarding address – my dear late husband worked in the university, as an administrator. I invited Andrew's sister to come back to me if she didn't get any joy out of the university but she didn't return, so I can only assume she made progress.'

Hennessey was shown out by the housekeeper, who before she closed the door behind him said, 'She's in dreadful pain, you know, arthritis, but you'd never guess if you didn't know her. She just refuses to give in.'

It happened as it always seemed to happen, an unexpected sight of something that triggered the memory. Usually it was the glimpse of a motor-cyclist through the windscreen of his car, often travelling at speed, crouching low over the fuel tank of the machine to reduce wind resistance, but on this occasion it was different. On this occasion it was more poignant. Hennessey had left the Wall household and turned right to walk up Victoria Road to reach the university as directed. He crossed a side street, and as he stepped into the road he glanced up the street. There at the kerb was a young man lavishing love, care and attention on a motor cycle, and suddenly Hennessey was eight years old again, helping Graham polish his beloved Triumph as it stood on its rest against the kerb outside their parents' little terrace house in Colomb Street, Greenwich. And he remembered how Graham would take him for a spin, round Blackheath Common, or across Tower Bridge to Trafalgar Square and back. Then there was that day, that night, that fateful, horrible night when he lay in bed listening to Graham leave the house, kick his machine roaring into life, listened as Graham rode away down Trafalgar Road, climbing through the gears. He lay there straining to catch every last decibel until all sound of Graham's bike had been swallowed by the other noises of the night: the ships on the river, the other traffic on Trafalgar Road, the drunken Irishman who walked beneath his window chanting his 'Hail Mary's. Hennessey remembered many details of that night, because later on there was a light but authoritative tap on the door, *tap, tap – tap*, the policeman's knock, which he would come to use . . . the sound of voices, his mother wailing . . . his father coming to his room, fighting back his own tears, to tell him that Graham had ridden to heaven, 'to save a place for us'. And later, a few days later, the funeral: the coffin being lowered, and on such a fine summer's day, with birds singing and butterflies flitting through the air. George Hennessey saw then that summer is not the time for a funeral, when all about is green and in full bloom and the sun is high and strong, that that is not the time for a man to die. And no season is the right time to die when one is only eighteen years old. Life, from that moment on, had seemed incomplete. Whereas, before that terrible time, there had been somebody ahead of him, someone to look up to, someone to follow, after that time there had just been a void. Even now, close to the end of his working life, George Hennessey still felt the emptiness where an older brother should be. And all his life he had failed to understand humankind's love affair with the car or motor cycle. Whether two wheels or four, both, so far as he believed, were the most dangerous machines ever invented. And could he walk up to that young man, polishing his machine, and say, 'No, don't get on it'? You cannot tell youth anything; as the car sticker says, HIRE A TEENAGER WHILE THEY STILL KNOW

EVERYTHING, because the young man does not believe he can be killed. For him, as for all youth, death is something that happens to others. It won't happen to him. Hennessey walked on.

Following the directions given to him by Mrs Wall's housekeeper, he turned right at the top of Victoria Road and continued to walk towards the city centre with Woodhouse Moor on his right, and came, at the next set of traffic lights, to the unmissable university. He enquired of likely-looking people and eventually found the offices of the Faculty of Accountancy.

'Doubt if we could help you.' The administrative officer was polite, warm, efficient. 'We would only keep a note of our alumni's address and class of degree awarded.'

'If you could check the address? The name is Quinlan, Andrew, and he would have joined the university about thirty years ago.'

'We record by date of graduation, so I'll check twenty-seven years ago. Quinlan. If you'd care to take a seat, I'll be as speedy as I can.' Hennessey sat in the chair indicated, and glanced out through a wide window to white buildings of angular concrete-and-glass design. Very 'space-age', very twentieth-century. The room itself was decorated in pastel shades, with exotic plants in very dry pots. The administrative assistant returned looking pleased with herself and holding a piece of notepaper. Hennessey stood.

'278 Brudenell Road,' she said. 'That's very near here. I can give you directions.'

'Thank you.'

The administrator glanced at the notepaper she held. 'He took a first.'

'Did he now?'

'Oh yes, according to his records. You're trying to trace him, you say?'

'Yes.'

'Well, the Institute of Chartered Accountants might help you; they keep a register of all CAs. They probably won't release the details without a court order, but they may be prepared to contact him and ask him to contact you. That's if he's in the UK. A first in accountancy from this university is a very saleable qualification globally, so he could be anywhere in the world.'

'I see; that's one avenue I could explore.' Hennessey paused. 'Would anyone here in this department remember him? Does any member of staff still teach that taught here when Quinlan was a student?'

'Dr Folding – he would remember him, I'm sure. I think all other staff joined within the last twenty years.'

'Andrew Quinlan, that's a name from way back. But yes, I remember Andy. I wasn't much older than him then. My, have I been with this department thirty years or more?' Dr Folding was a short, rotund figure with silver hair. His office was kept immaculately tidy. 'He took a first, you know. That's the nature of teaching: you remember the good ones and you remember the bad ones, but the middling ones you don't remember. But Andrew, one of the good ones. Yes, I can still remember him – short, finely made guy; a bit retiring, timid; threw himself into his studies. His mates threw themselves into the bar, and had to work at exam time, but Andrew wasn't a social animal. Bit of a hanger-on, really. I have a photograph of his year group.' Folding stood and reached for a photograph album that rested on a shelf. 'Keep photographs of 'em all. Started it the year before Andrew came up to the university, continued it ever since. Photograph the year group upon joining.' Folding resumed his seat and turned to the front of the album, then handed it to Hennessey.

'That's Quinlan's year group, the second photograph down, and that . . .' Folding leaned over the album and with a ballpoint pointed to a lanky-looking, bespectacled, dark-haired youth at the end of the second line of students, 'that is Andrew Quinlan.'

'So that's him.'

'That's how he *was*. Now, if he's still with us, he'll be podgy with good living, as all accountants and solicitors are. He was eighteen, nineteen then, now he'll be in his fifties. So your guess as to his current appearance is as good as mine. But that photograph does tell you about his personality. We don't place people for their photograph, just put a row of chairs out, invite people either to sit on a chair or stand behind. I'm no psychologist but I have noticed that the ones who have a sense of worth, or even self-importance, go for the chairs, and as near the centre as they can. Those who have a sense of humility or modesty, or lack of self-esteem, gravitate to the standing line, as near to the edge as possible. And look where Quinlan put himself, standing at the edge.'

'So I see.' Hennessey's eye was drawn to a well-built young man sitting in the centre of the front row. He had cold, piercing eyes. 'Quite the opposite to *him*, in fact.'

'Him?'

Hennessey pointed to the young man in the centre of the front row.

'Oh . . . you remember the good ones and you remember the bad ones. That was an arrogant piece of work. Now he was called . . . called . . . excuse me, can I take the album?' Folding took the album from Hennessey, removed the photograph from its corner mountings and read the reverse. 'Oh yes, Drover, how could I forget that? Clement Drover. He was a Drover of the brewery firm, Drover's Ales.' He replaced the photograph. 'He failed his degree, disappeared into the ether. Doubtless went back to the family firm and was accommodated, employment-wise. It's interesting you should notice him, because he and Andrew Quinlan became friends, shared a house together. I think Andrew was awed and impressed by Drover, but I worried for Andrew; I thought he was easily led and was getting into bad company . . . But I feared for nothing, because he got his first.'

'Do you know where he went after leaving Leeds?'

'Do you know, I think I do . . . I remember giving this information to a lady who came looking for him. She said she was his sister, and I believed her.' He leaned forwards and picked up the phone on his desk. He pressed two buttons and when his call was answered he said, 'Mrs Watson, the file on Andrew Quinlan – can you access it again? There'll be a copy of the reference we wrote for him. Can you let me know which firm he applied for a job with, please?' He replaced the phone.

They waited for about ninety seconds. Folding picked up the phone, said, 'Hi,' listened, wrote on a notepad, then said, 'Many thanks,' and replaced the phone.

'A firm called Vernon and Scott and Company, Selby.' Folding handed Hennessey a piece of notepaper. 'He must have got the job because he only asked us for the one reference.'

'Thanks.' Hennessey copied the name on to his notepad. 'Tell me, would you say that Andrew Quinlan had what you might call public-school mannerisms?'

'Oh, not at all. Not very polished at all, really – but I liked him, very sincere bloke – but he may have now, thirty years an accountant, those manners will rub off on you. He could be really quite polished now.'

Hennessey followed the administrative officer's directions to Brudenell Road and found that he was effectively

139

retracing his steps. Brudenell and Victoria Roads were practically parallel with each other and just a few hundred feet apart. Number 278 was run down, with a small front garden in which domestic refuse and beer cans, pizza plates and hamburger containers had been allowed to accumulate. He stepped up to the front door, pressed the bell and heard the *ding dong, ding dong* echo inside the building. The door was opened by a cheery girl in jeans and a woollen jumper. 'Hi,' she smiled.

'Hi,' Hennesey responded. 'Police.' He showed his ID. 'I take it this is a student house?'

'Yes.'

'Absentee landlord?'

'Yes.'

'Who is . . . ?'

'Which is, really. It's a business more than a landlord. It's called Leeds and Bradford Rents.'

'Leeds and Bradford Rents,' Hennessey repeated.

'They have an office at Hyde Park traffic lights.' She pointed up Brudenell Road towards Woodhouse Moor. 'Turn left at the top, come to the traffic lights, it's to the left of the pub amongst the parade of shops.'

'Thanks.'

'We have property in both cities. All let to students. It's good business. They always move and they always pay. Nice number to be in.' The man at Leeds and Bradford Rents leaned back in his chair. He was in his twenties, with a gold watch and expensive jewellery on his fingers. Behind him the wall was adorned with photographs of houses, all save one or two with small circular red stickers in the bottom right-hand corner. Hennessey presumed that the sticker indicated the property had been let. If it meant the opposite, then the company was in trouble.

'I'm interested in the property at Brudenell Road.'

'We have a few down there.'

'278.'

'Oh, yes.'

'How long have you owned the property?'

'Not long. About four or five years. Came on the market when the previous landlord died and his estate was sold off. He owned ten houses. His beneficiaries clearly didn't know what a nice little earner they were selling. They were run down and we bought them for a song. He wasn't getting the most out of them, only four students in that property when we bought it. We've divided up the rooms, there's eight in there now. Stretches the fire regulations a bit, but doesn't break them. For the lay-out of a few sheets of hardboard, a little bit of paint and some electrical knick-knacks we doubled the income in that property.'

Hennessey did not find it difficult to see where the young man's jewellery came from. 'So you have no idea who was living there thirty years ago?'

'Ha!' The young man laughed. 'No way. No way at all.'

'I knew it was a long shot, but they've paid off before.'

'Your only hope is the city library, centre of the town, as you'd expect. A lot of students register to vote at their university address. If you ask me, it's a statement about leaving home. If the occupants of 278 Brudenell Road did that thirty years ago, the library will have the voters' roll in their archives.'

Hennessey forgave the young man his jewellery.

'Thirty years? No problem.' The lady in the Local Studies section to which Hennessey had been directed smiled

141

confidently at his request. 'We go back to the old parish Burghers' Rolls, in fact, which preceded the present electoral roll. Do you know the ward?'

'Well the address is Brudenell Road, number 278.'

'Headingley South. I live in that ward myself. If you'd like to take a seat?'

Hennessey sat and enjoyed the building. Nineteenth-century, built as part of the Victorian Civic Pride move-ment, when cities in the north tried to outdo each other with buildings designed to evoke Augustan-era splendour. As the story had been related to him, the city fathers of Leeds had waited until Bradford had built its town hall, then had theirs designed so that it was one foot wider and one foot taller than Bradford's. His own particular favourite example of Civic Pride in the north of England was the façade of Huddersfield railway station: neat, proud, magnificent. It could easily be the façade of a stately home. And the building in which he presently sat was clearly of that era – stone-built with arched windows, the woodwork of tables and shelves clearly the work of craftsmen carpenters – and it had the silence and solemnity of all libraries.

The electoral roll for Headingly South of thirty years previously was contained in a large, leather-bound volume which the librarian, holding it in both hands, handed to Hennessey. 'I've dusted it down,' she explained, 'but it's still a bit mucky.'

Hennessey carried it to a nearby table, drew a scowl from an elderly dog-collared cleric as he placed it opposite the man on the table, and began to leaf through the pages. Thirty years ago, four people had registered to vote at the address 278 Brudenell Road: Andrew Quinlan, Simon Inglish, Thomas Gibbon and Clement Drover. And of those names it was 'Clement Drover' that seemed to leap off the page at him. Clement Drover, who was sufficiently full of himself to sit at the centre of the front row of the year-group photograph and yet who had insufficient about him, in terms of application or brainpower, to pass the course. He took a note of the names and returned the roll to the enquiry desk, with thanks.

It had, he thought, been a very successful afternoon, though a trifle foot-wearying. Rather than return speedily to York via Crossgates, he chose the slower, scenic route, relaxing as the train crossed over the beauty of Wharfedale basking in the late-April sun, and enjoying the view of the gorge at Knaresborough. For his money, of the two rail links between York and Leeds the Harrogate line was infinitely preferable, and he never tired of it.

At York he walked the short distance from the station to Micklegate Bar Police Station. He signed in at the enquiry desk, checked his pigeonhole and then walked to his office to write up his afternoon's work in the steadily growing file on Amanda Dunney, now cross-referred to the file on Andrew Quinlan.

He drove home, just catching the last of that evening's rush-hour, and arrived at his four-bedroom detached house on the Thirsk Road in Easingwold at approximately 6 p.m. He smiled with pleasure as he approached his house and saw a silver BMW parked on the verge. He turned into his driveway and parked in front of his garage.

Charles Hennessey leaned on the fence that ran between the house and the garage and served to confine Oscar to the garden and house in George Hennessey's absence. Father and son smiled and nodded to each other as Hennessey senior got out of his car, and Oscar ran in circles on the lawn, barking with joy.

'Still a few blanks, I see.' Charles Hennessey looked at the sheet of paper that lay on the tabletop as George

Hennessey poured boiling water from the kettle into the teapot.

'Yes, just five or six, I think. Strange, the same thirty-plus names were shouted out each weekday morning in termtime for five years, give or take the occasional departure and late arrival. You'd think I could remember them, but about six elude me.'

'You're too hard on yourself, Dad.' Charles smiled as George joined him at the kitchen table, carrying a tray of tea and a plate of biscuits.

'Have to keep the grey cells active. What's your news?'

'Children are well, thank you; they're off to their other grandparents this coming weekend. That should give me a chance to paint the patio doors. That's one job that is hugely outstanding.'

'Home ownership is a series of jobs; one follows another.'

'So I'm finding.'

'How's work?' Hennessey poured the tea.

'Plenty coming in at the moment. I seem to be in demand. I'm in Hull this week, thankfully going G to a serious assault which took place in front of plenty of witnesses. It's the only thing he can do, throw himself at the mercy of the court, but he'll collect anything up to five years.'

'That serious an assault?'

'It was very serious. Put the other fellow in hospital for a long time and with permanent physical damage, with the possibility of brain damage emerging later. My client's problem is that he just can't keep his fists to himself, nor can he control his temper. He has a string of previous, nothing psychiatrically wrong with him – that defence has been well explored – and he's going in front of a hanging judge.'

'I see.'

'So there's little I can do for him, and he knows it. He knows the form, knew the wisdom of going G. without me advising him. A pubload of witnesses, for heaven's sake, no provocation, just didn't like the look of his victim. He'll come out, then do it again, then go inside and come out and do it yet again – in-out, in-out, in-out – and then when he's in his forties he'll burn out and take an allotment.'

'Tell me the old story. Keeps us both in employment, though. I nail 'em and you get 'em off.'

'Not this time. But I find something honest about this man: he acts before he thinks, but will plead guilty if he is guilty. Far better than the people who'll swear blind that they didn't commit the crime in question, despite overwhelming evidence to the contrary, even managing to convince themselves of their own innocence. Insisting on going N.G. in the face of evidence like that is only going to invite a very heavy sentence. But will they listen?'

'Will they ever?' Hennessey stood on the veranda at the rear of his house, looking out over the back garden as soft rain fell vertically. The garden had been designed by Jennifer when she was heavily pregnant with Charles. They were still newly-weds when they bought the house. It had a dull garden, just a square front lawn and a large rectangular patch of grass at the rear of the house. One evening, when her condition precluded her from doing any physical work, she had sat down, pen and paper in hand, and designed the back garden. The large, rectangular lawn, she decided, would have to be divided widthways by a privet, and set in the middle of the privet would be a wrought-iron gate. Beyond the privet, the garden shed or sheds would be placed, and apple trees planted. Beyond the apple trees would be an area of waste ground, or 'going forth' as she had called it, having read the term in Francis Bacon's essay 'Of Gardens'. The 'going forth', she decided, would be a band of uncultivated land, about fifteen feet wide, in which a pond should be dug to attract amphibia. And the young George Hennessey, newly promoted to the rank of Detective Constable and thrilled by the prospect of parenthood, had dutifully set about creating a back garden to his wife's design. She had yet, she had said, to turn her thoughts to the front garden.

Then she had died. When Charles, born of a speedy and uncomplicated delivery, was just three months old. Standing there, watching the rain fall on the garden, Jennifer's garden, he thought about her death.

It had been a summer's day, in the afternoon. She was in the centre of Easingwold, just another young housewife doing a little shopping, when she collapsed. Folk rushed to her aid, thinking she had fainted, but no pulse was to be found and she was pronounced 'condition black' upon arrival at the hospital or, as used to be the term, 'dead on arrival'. No illness, no injury, no poisonous substances in her system . . . all the doctors could offer by means of explanation was the diagnosis of 'sudden death syndrome'. It really spoke of ignorance on the part of the medical profession who could offer no explanation as to why life should suddenly leave a healthy young woman. Over the years he had read small 'fillers' in newspapers reporting the sudden and unexplained death of a young person, and he knew what grief, what profound sense of unfairness, lay behind each article.

And, like Graham, Jennifer had died in the summer, and Hennessey once again saw the incongruity of summertime funerals. Unlike Graham, Jennifer was cremated, and Hennessey scattered her ashes over her garden; and each day, no matter what the weather, if he was at home he would talk to her, tell her of his day. 'Will they ever listen?' he said again. 'But it keeps me in a job. Charles visited but he's left, doing well now. He's pleased for me in respect of my lady-friend, as I know you are. You must know that I still and always will burn a candle for you, dear heart; I know you understand. I sense that you're pleased for me.'

He returned inside the house, made a meal, a filling and wholesome casserole, after which he took Oscar for his walk. He read a chapter of an obscure but entertaining book about the Peninsular War and then strolled into Easingwold for a pint of stout at the Dove Inn, just the one before last orders were called.

Seven

*In which Hennessey and Yellich hear of 'the Cuckoo'
and another shallow grave is discovered*

THURSDAY 7–FRIDAY 8 APRIL

D irectory Enquiries gave him the number and Hennessey and phoned it.

'Institute of Chartered Accountants.' The receptionist's voice, it seemed to Hennessey, to belong to a highly educated young woman; he thought it had more depth somehow than was usual amongst telephonists. 'How may I help you?'

'Police in York speaking.'

'Yes, sir.'

'We are trying to trace up to four chartered accountants.'

'Yes, sir.'

'I was wondering if you could help us?'

'If you give me their names, I will tell you if they are registered and what is their place of work.'

'It's as easy as that?' Hennessey was genuinely surprised.

'It's as easy as that. It's public knowledge, you see: the public library in York will have a copy of the register, anyone can access it, but I have the latest edition with me now, I'm actually holding it.'

148

'Excellent.' Hennessey turned to the notes he had made the day before in the Local Studies section of Leeds City Library. 'The names are Andrew Quinlan, Simon Inglish, Clement Drover and Thomas Gibbon.'

'OK.' The telephonist paused, and Hennessey heard the unmistakable sound of pages being turned as a book was leafed through. 'Well, there is only one Thomas Gibbon registered; he is in Tiverton, Devon, Bookman and Company . . . No one of the name Drover is registered . . .'

'Figures.'

'Why?'

'He failed his exams.'

'Oh, well, he wouldn't be registered then.'

'Just double-checking, he could have got them at a later date, second attempt.'

'Of course. The other two names . . . yes, Andrew Quinlan is registered, he is with Vernon and Scott and Company, Selby; and the final name, Inglish . . . Yes, Simon Inglish, he's up in your neck of the woods as well, he is with Felling and Company, offices in Malton.'

'Could you give me their address and phone number, please?'

'Quinlan, Drover and Gibbon.' Simon Inglish smiled. 'Sounds like a firm of solicitors or accountants, hard to imagine us then becoming what we have become – well, three of us. Poor old Clement, bombed his finals. Never knew what became of him; I lost contact with the other two, but I follow their progress through the membership directory of the Institute.' Simon Inglish seemed to have done well out of accountancy; he was comfortably middle-aged, in expensive-looking suit and silk shirt. A short man, he was clean-shaven as Hennessey noticed was the norm amongst accountants, with a full head of blond hair, neatly trimmed. He worked in an oak-panelled office with low beams and a view from his window of fields and woodland. 'How on earth did you know we shared a house together?'

'Voters' roll, it's still held in the Leeds Library.'

'Ah . . . they keep the roll, don't they, very useful to historians, valuable archive.'

'There were just four of you in the house?'

'Yes, we four. It was our final year, we'd had enough of halls of residence by then. We wanted the independence and privacy of a shared rented house.'

'I can understand that. So, tell me about Andrew Quinlan.'

'Andy . . . intelligent, even for an undergraduate; he was intelligent and hard-working. He got a first. Not bad. I was lazy and only managed a third. Tom Gibbon wing-and-prayered himself to a 2:2, he was a chancer. I was hard-working compared to Tom, but Tom had cracked "exam technique", as it's known, get little out of the course but you get the bit of paper; and Clement didn't manage anything at all. But Andy, what can I tell you about him?'

'Anything you like.'

'Trying to get the measure of him?'

'As he was then.'

'Well . . . he and Clement Drover spent a lot of time together, they hit it off. They had a lot of differences but one huge thing in common, which is that they were both alone in life.'

'Oh?'

'Yes, they felt they'd been abandoned by their families, as I recall. Other than that they were very different. Different backgrounds, different appearance; at that age people usually make friends with people who remind them of themselves, have you noticed? Two tall men will hit it off, but not usually a tall man and a short man; two attractive women will team up together, but not an attractive one and a plain one. Two people from public-school backgrounds will become friends but rarely an ex-public-school boy and a council-educated "oik". In my observation, friendships among people with differences like that come later in life.'

'I wouldn't disagree with that.' Hennessey nodded. He thought it a reasonable social observation.

'But Andy and Clement were the exception. Clement was tall and handsome and ex-public school; Andy was short, not a success with the girls, and had grown up in a children's home. Yet I think, had one been a woman, a marriage would have resulted.'

'I see.'

'Andrew was the needier of the two. He seemed to latch on to Clement. When they walked up to the Hyde Park for a beer, Andy seemed to be half a step behind Clement. Andy worked, Clement enjoyed much help from him, to the point of copying Andy's work, so as to produce termwork.'

'Oh . . .'

'You don't do that at university. I think Clement got dependent on Andy as a workhorse, and Andy seemed to look up to Clement as a source of answers for life's problems. He was impressed by Clement's charm, his way with words, his social grace, none of which Andy had.'

'And Clement felt abandoned in life, you say?'

'Yes. He was adopted. You know the brewers, Drover's Ales?'

'Oh, yes.'

'He was adopted into that family – doing their bit to salve their social conscience, I should think. Good for them, you might say, but they treated him right cruelly.'

'Oh?'

'Well – and this is his side of the story, you understand?'

'Accepted.'

'Might be a wholly different version to be had from the Drover family.'

'Understood.'

'Well, they brought him up as one of theirs: expensive education, lovely house to live in, holidays on the west coast of Scotland in the family yacht, told him he was adopted at an early age – that was the right thing to do – but when he was eighteen, he was told that was it.'

'It?'

'He was on his own. They shut the door on him at eighteen, cut him off without a penny. They felt they had done their job by providing him with a privileged childhood, that it had earned them a place in heaven, but because he wasn't blood family, at the age of eighteen he was left to his own devices. He said it would have been better if he hadn't been adopted by them. But to allow him to live that lifestyle, then see their job done the moment he's eighteen, no share of the family fortune, not even a bit of cash to get started, a job in the firm . . . ? Don't make me laugh. He went from the Drovers' palatial home to drawing dole and living in a bedsit.'

'But he got to university?'

'It was his only way forward. He knew he had to get an education, get qualified. He told me he wanted to be an accountant because you never meet a poor accountant. That was his motivation, not a fascination with figures and the tax law maze, which drives most of us. He had his pre-university entrance qualifications courtesy of his expensive schooling, so the Drovers at least gave him that leg-up. He had that to thank them for.'

'It was something, I suppose.' Hennessey shifted his position in the chair.

'But I still think he felt more resentment towards them than gratitude, just being cut off at the age of eighteen for no other reason than that he wasn't a blood relative. They had a very superficial appreciation of what adoption means.'

'Did it for themselves, rather than for him?'

'That's a neat way of putting it, but you understand that I am only repeating what Clement said about himself. He could easily have been cut off following his attempted embezzlement of the family fortunes, or something which was kept hushed up.'

'Could easily have been,' Hennessey conceded. 'It's not unknown for adoptees to turn against their adopters for no logical reason. What they say about the kid and the ghetto holds much water in my experience.'

'"You can take a kid out of the ghetto, but you'll never take the ghetto out of the kid"?'

'That's the one. You adopt a child, you also adopt whatever damage has been done to him or her prior to your good intentions being realised.'

'I don't think I could do it. Never given it any thought, having three beautiful children of my own. You any family?'

'One son. He's a lawyer, a barrister.'

'I see. I would have settled for two, but my wife wanted a third. There's quite an age gap between number one son, number two son and number one daughter, but Gillian got broody when age was becoming a crucial issue . . . Anyway, she lets me think that I'm the head of the household but she always seems to get what she wants.'

Hennessey smiled. He thought Inglish fortunate to have had the option. 'I think I'd like to talk to the Drover family. As you say, there might be a story there that has to be told.'

'So is Clement in trouble with the law?'

'We don't know yet, Mr Inglish. But we might ask him to help us with our enquiries.'

'As they say!'

'So when did you last see Clement Drover?'

'The summer after finals. He was not a happy man. We other three had graduated, looking forward to our years of advancement – ten, fifteen, even the next twenty years, so that your career consolidates when you're in your forties. The degree is just the beginning really – 'Your finals are your beginning', as we were told. But we were quite cock-a-hoop, especially Andy Quinlan with his first. Poor old Clement drowning his sorrows in booze and one or two illicit substances.'

Hennessey raised his eyebrows.

'A little cannabis, a snort of coke . . . we were still students.' Inglish paused. 'You know, Clement showed another side of himself at that point. He became surly, cynical, very resentful towards us, but towards Andy in particular. I think he felt he should have had his degree for the asking, not in reward for work. I think he resented Andy quite a lot, because for three years the two of them had been mates, but Andy was always the junior partner in the relationship, and at the end of it all it was Andy that got the good degree. While Drover the magnificent, who bossed Andy about, who made the decisions, who got the girls—'

'He failed.'

'Yes. Never knew what happened to him.'

'When did you last see him?'

'When I left the house. I went back to live with my parents in Hampshire, but couldn't settle in the south.

After any length of time in the hard north you feel that the south of England is false somehow; life has a softness down there.'

'I'm a Londoner, and I wouldn't call London soft, but I know what you mean: all those thatched roofs in a patchwork of fields, clean air, no factories spewing out sulphur, no coalmines or canals full of rusting pram frames.' Hennessey grinned. 'I just love the north.'

'So, Drover stayed on in your shared house?'

'Yes. As did Andy Quinlan. They negotiated with the landlord for an extended let. It suited the landlord really, because it kept the house occupied over the summer – less vulnerable to burglary, you see. Nothing to steal in there anyway, but that won't put the bandits off. Andy and Clement still had that one thing in common, you see: neither had a home to go to. When I left, Andy was working in a pub, pulling pints to give himself an income while writing off for jobs with firms of accountants. Drover was drawing the dole and loafing about the house all day, getting drunk when he had the money to buy booze. And that's the last I saw of either of them.'

Hennessey thanked Simon Inglish for his time and for his information. He drove back to York a worried man. An awful realisation was dawning.

'Father was an odd fish.' Carolyne Drover sat impassively in a high-backed chair. Hennessey sat in a chair opposite Miss Drover; Yellich chose the settee, which stood a reverential distance from the two chairs at either side of the hearth, where a small coal fire burned. 'An odd fish indeed.' She leaned forwards, picked up a pair of tongs and lifted a piece of coal on to the fire. 'Just enough to keep me from feeling chilly,' she explained. 'Can't heat a house of this size with coal fires alone. The central heating comes on in the evening.'

'I see.' Hennessey smiled, and pondered that it was odd that Carolyne Drover had chosen to sit with her back to the window, so that when she looked up she saw the opposite wall, on which portraits hung. Hennessey on the other hand could look beyond Miss Drover, out through one of the two twelve-foot-high windows to the landscaped gardens at the rear of the house. 'You were saying?'

'Father, yes . . .' Carolyne Drover had pleasant, balanced features. Hennessey found her handsome in a feminine way, and wondered why she had never married. She would, he thought, have been a very attractive woman in her youth, and with the fortune she offered. 'He was a man of many parts, and those parts often contradicted each other. Cautious one minute, reckless the next; one minute in his element relishing the snakepit of politics of the business – you know, there's nothing more guaranteed to make blood relatives hate each other than a family business – and the next wanting only solitary pursuits. I can still picture him in the garden in a sunhat, sitting in front of his easel, not at all interested in this merger or that expansion, yet the next day he would be in the boardroom, thumping the table.'

'And Clement?'

'Clement was just one example of his contradictions. Father was very selfish, very jealous of the family. He had a very guarded attitude to his wife and children, me and my two brothers – very careful about whom we visited and who visited us. And then one day over breakfast he announced that we were going to adopt a child.'

'Just like that?'

'I can still sense Mother's disapproval. She kept quiet at the announcement, but it did come as a surprise to her. So she and Father talked, or rather argued, about it. Then it was our turn to be vetted, by the Social Services. There are obstacles to adoption, rightly so. We were all talked to by a female social worker who visited over a period of weeks, looked over the house . . . She was very impressed, but those people don't earn any money, so her own home must have been quite small. Anyway, a little later on Clement came for a few visits, then he moved in. He was six years old, very nervous.'

'Quite old to be adopted.'

'Yes, he was very lucky. Usually adopters want infants in cribs, a personality that can be moulded as their own children's personalities would be moulded, so six, yes, that was pushing it a bit, so lucky lad he.'

The fire spat. 'I think the coal merchant has mixed a bit of poor-quality stuff with the last delivery,' Carolyne Drover said by way of explanation and apology. 'I'll mention it to him. If it occurs again, we'll change our suppliers. I confess I do love a live fire, not just a live fire but a coal fire. Coke doesn't have the same character at all.'

'I live in a smokeless zone.' Hennessey sat deeper in the chair. 'I have to use coke.'

'So do we, really.' Carolyne Drover raised her eyebrows. 'But if you live in a large house, a long way from the nearest road, you can be a little naughty.'

She was dressed in a tartan skirt, a cream blouse and a red shawl, and seemed to Hennessey to blend with the room – its bookcase, its wood panelling – and her delicate scent mixed well with the smell of wood polish. Hennessey pondered the dreadful crimes that had been committed in remote houses and thought: More than a little naughty, madam. You can be downright evil if you've a mind.

'But to return to Clement. He was a very difficult boy, really tested the family, but Father never raised a hand to him, which was another example of his contrary nature. He is remembered as a strict disciplinarian, but he'd let Clement get away with murder. He was abandoned.'

'Clement?'

'Yes. Terrible story. Just four years old and his mother just walked out on him, locked the door behind her and walked away. He was alone in that house for two days, so we later found out. Apparently a neighbour saw him standing at the window, and didn't think much of it, but she saw him again six hours later, still standing at the window as if waiting for someone to return. She knocked on the door, couldn't get an answer, called the police, and little Clement Boyce went into care.'

'Horrible story.'

'It is, isn't it? He was two years in a succession of foster homes and children's homes before we adopted him. I never knew why we adopted him – I don't mean Clement particularly, but why Father would want to adopt at all.' Carolyne Drover leaned forward again, this time to pick up the poker, with which she stirred the coals. 'We never were offered an explanation for that. Anyway, Clement couldn't bear being left alone, especially in the early years, and thought he was being abandoned when he wasn't. By the time he was a teenager, we used to dread him coming home from school. He'd just suck out of the family, demand and demand and demand, break things, bully my younger brother, but complained like mad if my older brother thumped him. He wanted, and got, expensive things. My poor mother despaired but Father was adamant, he said you can't unadopt once you've adopted, that was it, no going back. Mother eventually began to refer to Clement as "the Cuckoo". We were walking one winter's day, a clean, crisp day, by the river, and she said, "We've taken a cuckoo into our nest." And I saw the image in my head, Clement pushing the natural children to one side, growing enormous, his beak permanently open, and Father just feeding him goodies. It's an image that stays with me to this day.'

'What became of him eventually?'

'That I don't know, Chief Inspector, and if you do locate him I would be interested to find out.'

'But he left the family.'

'It's our skeleton in the closet.' She fixed Hennessey with a stare, and held a silence. 'It was Father's policy to introduce the boys to the world of business, the family business. I was to marry and make my own way, doubtless with a generous dowry, but to marry out none the less.' She paused again. 'I did meet a man. We were soulmates, we could communicate by being quiet, you know, sitting in silence but still understanding each other . . . He was drowned. He went white-water rafting in Austria. He . . . well . . .'

'I'm sorry.'

'There was just never anyone else after that. Plenty of offers, some genuine, some nakedly greedy for Father's money, but no one could replace Julian. I could not give myself fully in marriage to another man, I would just have resented him for not being Julian. I would have resented our children for not being Julian's. I know myself well enough to know that I couldn't commit to another man, and going into marriage holding something back is not the correct attitude.'

'A brave decision, if I may say.'

'Fortunately, I had the means to make that decision, financially speaking. Had I been born into poverty, and had I no qualifications, I might have had to accept a second-choice husband as a necessary means of survival. But that was not my lot, and so here I am, not unhappy, and with warm memories of a lovely man.'

Hennessey allowed a moment's pause and then asked about the aforementioned skeleton in the closet.

'Oh yes. Well, Clement, he had a tendency to steal, a sneak-thief, things would be noticed missing: bits of Mother's jewellery, items of value. Eventually Clement was suspected and Mother complained to Father, but Father was adamant that Clement should remain in the family.'

Father took the boys into the company, and Clement, at his own request, was allowed a job in Accounts; this was really no more than a summer-vacation job before he went to university. In short, he embezzled money.'

'Ah . . .'

'In essence, it was quite a simple . . . scam, is that the word?'

'It'll do,' Hennessey said softly.

'What he did was to open a business account with a bank, called it . . . something, but not his real or adoptive name, something like Yorkshire Stationery or some such, and he would invoice the company for large quantities of paper which were non-existent. Having a job in Accounts, he authorised cheques to his company. But he got greedy; our senior accountant made enquiries on his own and reported the matter to Father. That element of betrayal was the thing that reached Father. Clement was then eighteen years of age, so he was invited to leave the household.'

'Invited?'

'Told, then. He took it badly, saw it as yet another abandonment, but didn't see how he had brought it on himself. He attempted to rationalise it, saying that he was doing the job of an accountant but paid peanuts, and he only took what he thought was fair, so as to increase his income to that of an accountant.'

'I've come across that sort of thinking before,' Hennessey said. 'It's not uncommon among criminals; it's the sort of mentality that people subscribe to when they want to justify their actions – only burgling houses of people who have insurance, for example.'

'How could they know who's insured?'

'Exactly, but the assumption is that a large house is an insured house, and therefore it's all right to turn the windows.'

'A dangerous attitude.'

'Very. You can find justification for anything with that attitude.'

'Clement might have learned good manners and social graces from us and from his school, but that "survive at all costs" attitude, that "me alone against the world", that was in him when he came and it never left him. Adopting him was a disaster. With the benefit of hindsight and with all the advantage of middle age, I can see now that while we offered him acceptance, his attitude to the family was exploitative.'

'And he left?'

'Eventually, not without pleading for another chance, and putting on an impressive show of remorse, which cut no ice with Mother and Father, but yes, he went. Last seen heading east, to Leeds and a place on the university's accountancy course during which time he lived on a grant. From that point all contact was severed; we never heard from him again. And there was no sense of loss, no sense of a vacuum left behind in our family. He was part of our lives for twelve years and caused a lot of headaches, but he left nothing of himself behind. His engagement with our family was superficial, emotionally speaking. He came, he took, he went.'

'Not a good experience?'

'A sense of contamination, really, I suppose he left that behind.'

Driving back to York with Yellich at the wheel, Hennessey broke the silence. 'The man known as Quinlan by the BMW dealership . . .'

'Yes, boss?'

'How was he described, appearance-wise?'

'Tall, well built, light-coloured hair.'

'Personality?'

'Pukka, but he would chat to the crew, gave one mechanic some good advice about income for his later years. The mechanic spoke highly of him.'

'That's what I was afraid of.' Hennessey glanced to his left and followed the flight of a heron across a field towards a stream. 'Andrew Quinlan, you see, was short and dark-haired, without public-school manners because he had grown up in a children's home.'

'Oh no.'

'Oh yes.'

'So . . .'

'The last time Clement Drover and Andrew Quinlan were known to be together was when they stayed on for a few weeks in a terraced house in Leeds which they had shared with other undergraduates. The two others left after finals to return home, but Quinlan and Drover carried on living there. Then Quinlan got a job, and Drover seemed to disappear, having failed his degree. No one knew what became of him.'

'Solemn, boss. Very solemn.'

'So if we assume that Drover is a missing person . . .'

'Or Quinlan?'

'Yes, or Quinlan; one or the other is missing. We don't need to feed the information into H.O.L.M.E.S. to be told what to do.'

'We don't, do we, boss?'

'What's H.O.L.M.E.S.?' Sarah Yellich nestled into her husband as they sat together on the settee watching mid-evening television and sharing a bottle of wine.

'A computer program. It stands for Home Office Local Major Enquiry System. Feed in information about a crime and it will print out suggestions, the program being written on the basis of similar crimes that have been investigated. And the boss was right: we don't need to be told to look under the floorboards of the last known address of a missing person.'

'Is that what you'll be doing?'

'Yes, tomorrow. Courtesy call to the West Yorkshire Police – they'll have to be present, it's now their case as much as ours, joint-forces investigation. Our enquiries now point to a murder on their turf.'

Sarah shuddered. 'Such a young man . . . and all those years ago.'

Yellich held her tightly. She was finely built with short, dark hair; he felt for her vulnerability. He felt very, very protective of her. And also of his son, presently upstairs, sleeping soundly.

George Hennessey sat at home in front of a glowing coke fire, Oscar at his feet, reading further the account of the Peninsular War as he let his dinner settle. At 9 p.m. he closed the book and said, 'Walk?', to which Oscar responded with a bark and a run in tight circles. He took Oscar for a mile up the Thirsk Road to a small copse, and let him explore the copse for approximately fifteen minutes while he eyed the night sky, with clouds scudding across the moor, and thought, albeit without the practised eye of a countryman, that the weather would hold, that there would be no rain that night. He walked the mile home with Oscar, who was a more reluctant walking partner than he had been on the outward leg.

Ensuring that the mongrel had sufficient food and water to sustain him overnight, that the rear door was locked but the dog flap open, Hennessey packed an overnight bag and drove to Skelton, north of York. He parked his car at the kerb outside a half-timbered, mock-Tudor detached house. He walked up the gravel drive and the front door was opened before he knocked on it.

'You told me that gravel was the best burglar deterrent.' The slender woman gave a warm smile of welcome. 'And you were right.' She stepped aside as Hennessey entered the house and walked into the kitchen, where Diane and Fiona looked up and said hello to him once before readdressing harnesses and stirrups, all of which had to be soaped and polished.

'We're entering Samson in an event on Saturday,' Louise D'Acre explained, and turned to the sink, where the metal parts of the bridle were being washed. 'Help yourself to tea.'

Hennessey made himself a cup of tea and carried it through to the lounge, where shortly afterwards a worried-looking Daniel found him. Daniel carried a school exercise book and sought help with his maths homework. By making much use of the printed example and applying logic, Hennessey surprised himself by finding his way through the maze, and between them he and Daniel completed the assigned tasks successfully. Presently the house calmed down, the polished and soaped bridles were stacked in the hall, and the children ran backwards and forwards along the landing from their bedrooms to their bathroom (the house having two, one for adults and the other designated for the children's use), and then all was silent. Hennessey and Louise sat in the kitchen looking into each other's eyes until Hennessey broke the silence by saying, 'It's quietened down now; shall we go up?'

FRIDAY 8 APRIL

Hennessey and Yellich stood back and let the officers of the West Yorkshire Police lead. It was, after all, their case.

'I don't know . . .' the smoothly dressed, bejewelled man of Leeds and Bradford Rents stammered. 'I can't give you permission. I'll have to ask head office, and I'm sure they'll demand a warrant to enter the property.'

The senior of the two West Yorkshire detectives, a man who had introduced himself as Inspector Tom 'Pony' Shetland, reached into his inside jacket pocket and took out a folded piece of paper, which he dropped on to the young man's desk. 'Read and weep, sunshine,' he said, 'read and weep.'

'Do you have keys for the property?' asked Detective Sergeant Robert 'Bob' Sale, also of the West Yorkshire Police. 'Or do we kick the door in?' Sale had a cold, hard attitude, so Hennesey thought.

'No . . . there'll probably be students there to open the door for you, but we have spare keys.' He stood, walked to a metal filing cabinet and opened the doors to reveal many keys on many hooks, all neatly labelled in rows.

'Well, any resident in the house will have to find alternative accommodation, if we find what we think we are going to find. How many properties do you manage? Those keys . . .'

'Yes.' The man allowed his voice to fall away as a double-decker bus whined to a halt at the Hyde Park lights. 'This office, 150 properties, Bradford about the same, Sheffield and Hull about half that each, but we hope to expand in those cities.' He groped for a key.

'I bet you do,' Sale snarled. 'My eldest has just started at Manchester, and I've seen what she's paying for what. An awful lot for very little. Student letting is a very nice little earner if you haven't got a conscience.'

'I . . .' the young man stammered, but fell silent and handed the keys to Inspector Shetland.

In the car, Shetland said, 'Both mine went to university, that they had reasonable accommodation for reasonable rent.'

'Private landlord?' Sale asked. He was tall and slender.

'Yes.' Shetland was a man of bulk, but Hennessey and Yellich also found him warm and humorous. Hennessey found it easy to see them playing good cop/bad cop with a suspect. 'Fair rents for dry, safe houses.'

The car pulled up outside 278 Brudenell Road, and a van containing uniformed officers pulled up behind it. Shetland walked calmly and confidently up to the front door and knocked on it. He turned to Sale and then to Hennessey and Yellich. 'Only 10 a.m., it'll be a bit early for them, bless 'em. Just wait until they get into the world of work: they won't know what's hit 'em.' He banged on the door with his fist.

'Minute . . .' The voice came from deep within the terraced house and sounded frail and weak. And, as if keeping a promise, about sixty seconds later the door was opened by a pale, somewhat sickly-looking youth. He was barefoot and wore jeans and a T-shirt; he blinked at the officers from deep-set eyes under a mop of black hair.

166

'Police,' said Shetland.

'Oh, yes. What's it about?'

'We have a warrant to search this house.'

'Search? We don't do drugs, not in this house.'

'Relieved to hear it, son, but we aren't looking for drugs.'

'No?'

'No.' Shetland pushed past the youth and the other officers, plain-clothed and uniformed, followed him in.

'Please come in,' said the youth sarcastically as the officers walked past him.

Shetland walked down the hallway to what was clearly a communal area with a kitchen off. It was carpeted and had an armchair, a settee, a TV set, posters on the wall, overflowing ashtrays and mugs half full of cold coffee. Shetland turned to Sale: 'How's this compared to your daughter's lodgings?'

'S'good, wouldn't mind her in this.' Sale called back to the youth who stood in the hall surrounded, consumed even, by large men in blue uniforms. 'What do you pay for this, son?' The youth told him. 'That's less than what my daughter pays for a damp hen coop.' He looked round him. 'First day I get off, I'm going over there; sort something out for her.'

'Right. How many people in this house, son?'

'Eight.'

'All at home?'

'Friday . . . yes, think so. No, Clive would have stayed over at his girlfriend's. Me and six others right now.'

'Right. Well, go and wake the six others up, tell them to get their tails down here a.s.a.p.'

'Yes, sir.'

The youth ran up the stairs and Hennessey heard a voice say, 'What's up, Brian?'

Brian replied, 'The house is full of cops.'

'Oh no, my stuff!'

'Quiet,' said Brian. 'Help me wake the others.'

In the communal room Shetland said, 'No drugs? Pulleth ye the other one, it jangles passing merrie.'

Presently all seven of those in residence stood in front of Tom Shetland, looking hungover and confused.

'Now listen.' Shetland spoke solemnly. 'I'm going to say this once; listen, do as you're told, do not ask a single question. Understand?'

The seven young people nodded.

'All right. Now this house is a crime scene. We have a warrant to search it, and search it we will. It is being searched in respect of a crime suspected of occurring thirty years ago, so none of you are suspects.'

There was an audible sigh of relief.

'What I want you to do is collect your belongings, as much as you can carry, and leave the house, because you won't be coming back here, not for a while. If any of you is a friend of "Clive" then collect his stuff as well and take it with you. Where you go, I don't care; you know your contacts, you know what the university accommodation people can do for you. You know what Leeds and Bradford Rents can do. It's likely that we'll be confining our search to the cellar, if this house has a cellar.'

'It has.' A tall youth pointed to the door behind Shetland.

'I see. Beneath the floorboards, the attic and the garden or back yard of this house. But we may also go in the upstairs rooms, so if you do have an illicit substance then take it with you. And that is the police doing you a favour in anticipation of your instant and unquestioning co-operation.'

The youths, clearly shaken, turned smartly to their right, like soldiers in obedience to some silent command, filed smoothly out of the room and ran up the stairs.

Half an hour later the police had total possession of the house.

'Well, gentlemen –' Shetland turned to the three plain-clothes officers – 'how shall we do this?'

'Let's not tear the house apart,' Hennessey said; 'that would be too clumsy. I suggest we look for some tell-tale sign of a body being concealed. If we don't find it, we might have to resort to tearing it apart.'

'A sign?'

'A patio that's not part of the original design, floor-boards that have been splintered at the sides or ends, a six-foot-long-one-foot-wide block of concrete . . . that sort of sign. Look in places where a body could be hidden, bricked-up cupboards, that sort of thing.'

'Done this before?' Shetland smiled.

'No.'

'Well, it makes sense anyway. Sergeant!'

'Sir.'

'Did you hear what Chief Inspector Hennessey just said?'

'Yes, sir.'

'Right. Organise your men; make sure they know what they're looking for.'

'Sir.'

Constables searched the attic, constables searched the cellar, but it was in the back garden that the body was found. A nervous and clearly shaken young constable entered the communal room and said, 'Excuse me, sir, gentlemen, but could you come outside? It just . . . well, it just looks like a grave.' And this not 120 seconds after the constables had been dispersed throughout the house.

The back garden was small and seemed to Hennessey to be a perfect square of about twenty feet by twenty. An old wooden shed stood to the left-hand side; it was beginning to rot – the felt on the roof had cracked; and a concrete path ran down the centre of the garden to the fence. The garden itself seemed to have been trampled into nothing more than two strips of new, naked soil either side of the pathway. A simple but effective barbecue made of loose house bricks and a grill covered with foil suggested the reason for the lack of vegetation. It was not difficult for the police to imagine well-attended cook-outs during the summer evenings, or parties that spilled out of the house and into the garden. Beside the barbecue was a strip of concrete, approximately six feet long and two feet wide, flush with the surface of the soil. In itself, thought Hennessey, it did not look suspicious. Each successive tenant of the house would have glanced at it once and then dismissed it. Plenty of youths down the years had probably stood or sat on it while tucking into their grilled sausages, yet look for a body somewhere on the premises and the patch of concrete seemed to shout loudly. Hennessey saw what the young constable meant: it did look just like a grave.

'We'll need a pneumatic drill,' Shetland said. 'Can you send for one please, Bob?'

When disintegrated by the drill, the concrete revealed itself to be two feet deep; it covered, rather than encased, a human form, wrapped in heavy-duty plastic sheeting, the sort Hennessey had noticed that builders often use to protect unfinished work from sudden downpours.

'Looks like your hunch was right, George.' Shetland smiled grimly, a grimace almost.

Hennessey nodded in response and allowed himself

time to wish that Shetland hadn't said 'hunch', disliking as he did the seemingly unstoppable encroachment, invasion even, of Americanisms into the Queen's English. 'Intuition' would have been better, even 'guess' would have been acceptable, but 'hunch', no. He was not sorry to see his retirement on the horizon. The day that British policemen had 'hunches' was the time for him to rent that allotment he had long promised himself. 'It will, I think,' he said as he looked at the still-shrouded object, 'transpire to be a male corpse, in his early twenties when he died. And if identification is possible, it will prove to be the body of Andrew Quinlan.'

'I'll phone for our scene-of-crimes people and the duty pathologist; they'll have to be here before we remove him. Poor lad.'

'It's a male skeleton, all right.' Hennessey looked into the grave. 'It would have foxed me if it was female, but it's not, and that's one step nearer to it being the skeleton of Andrew Quinlan.'

Hennessey could not help but notice the contrast. The pathology laboratory at York District Hospital, though well equipped, was modest by comparison to that at St James's in Leeds. Here were numerous stainless-steel tables, and a large glass screen ran the length of one wall of the room, beyond which were seats arranged in tiers, all at the moment empty. St James's was, after all, a renowned teaching hospital, the largest in Europe.

Hennessey stood in the obligatory green coveralls, attending the post-mortem at the invitation of Inspector Shetland. The pathologist was a clean-shaven man, who appeared to be in his early thirties, and was assisted by a short, slightly built laboratory technician. The fifth person in the room lay on the stainless-steel table, clearly human, clearly almost fully decomposed, a few shreds of very durable and resistant flesh preventing the remains from being fully skeletal.

The pathologist pulled the microphone, which was attached to an anglepoise arm, which in turn was attached to the ceiling, so that it remained above the table at a level with his mouth. 'The date is the eighth of April, the time is fourteen hundred hours. This is case number whatever on my list please, Susan – Dr Dunn, this is, in case you do not recognise my dulcet tones. So, to business. The body is that of a male, and an adult, but the sutures in the skull have not fully knitted, suggesting that he was less than twenty-five years old when he died. The body is in an advanced state of decomposition. All bones are present, no body part has been removed. There is no obvious sign of trauma to the body. Could you pass the tape measure please, Mr Ives?' Mr Ives took a retractable metal tape measure from the instrument trolley and handed it to the pathologist. 'The deceased,' Dunn spoke for the benefit of the microphone, 'was of short stature in life, measuring only five feet three or four inches in height, or about 160 centimetres in Eurospeak.' He looked across the room at the two police officers. 'I'm a Eurosceptic.'

'So am I,' Shetland and Hennessey, who stood close to each other, replied in unison, then turned and grinned at each other.

'Rabies and bankruptcy, that's what we'll get from being in Europe,' Hennessey whispered, respecting the sanctity of the pathology lab. 'The history of Europe is full of bilateral and multi-lateral trading agreements, some of which have lasted longer than the human lifespan, but all of which have been dissolved, and the European Union will be just another to add to the list. So my son said. He's a barrister.'

'Bloody Brussels, even told us what size desks we have to put our computers on.'

'Gentlemen, please.' Dunn raised an eyebrow. 'The tape recorder is very sensitive, it'll pick up even your hushed conversation. The odd aside is acceptable.'

The two officers fell silent, but Hennessey thought Dr Dunn's comment rich – he did start the discussion after all.

'Can't be more precise about the height because skeletons shrink as the cartilage contracts and the fleshy soles of the feet decay. But he was a short chap in life. The teeth are exposed and indicate that he was white European in terms of his ethnicity.' Dunn asked for a metal rod to be handed to him from the instrument trolley and this he forced between the upper and lower sets of teeth and prised the jaws apart. They gave with a loud *crack*. 'Yes . . . the teeth in fact confirm white European ethnic grouping . . . the Asian and Caucasian skulls are very similar, and easily mistaken for each other, but the teeth are different, and our friend here was Caucasian. He had had some dental work done – a filling here and there, very old dentistry, and probably from childhood, there's something worn about the fillings. I think he probably neglected his teeth towards the end of his life but they're all there. He hadn't lost a single tooth, indicating a young man.'

'Fitting the description?' Shetland hissed.

'Yes,' Hennessey nodded.

'I'll extract a tooth and do a cross-section; that'll give his age at death, plus or minus twelve months, but the presence of all his teeth reinforces the impression given by the skull not having fully knitted, that this man died very young, in his early twenties. If you know who his dentist was, his records may still be available; but I think this fella has been in the clay for a long time, and dentists are obliged to keep records for only eleven years after the patient's last treatment.'

'If it is who we believe it to be, he has been buried for about thirty years.' Hennessey spoke softly but clearly.

'Really? Rather pushing our luck in respect of dental records then, ain't we?' Dunn paused. 'I'll do what I can to assist in identification, but a lot of effort appears to have gone into hindering that.'

'Oh?'

'He appears to have been naked when he was buried. There are no remains of any form of textile, no matter how rotted, but had he been buried in clothing I would have expected to find non-perishable items – zip fasteners, buttons – among the "remains", bra suspender hooks in the case of a female corpse.'

'Not exclusively female,' Shetland said, and Hennessey allowed himself a brief chuckle. Dr Dunn and Mr Ives also shared the joke, and the solemnity of the proceedings was briefly lifted.

'So . . .' Dr Dunn pondered the corpse, drumming his fingers on the rim of the stainless-steel table as he did. 'So, what did kill you, my friend? Speak to me. Hello? . . .' He leaned forward and asked for a pair of tweezers to be handed to him. Holding the tweezers delicately, he poked into the ribcage of the skeleton. 'Unless I am mistaken, this is a maggot cocoon. Laid by a fly, a common housefly. It points to the death taking place during the summer months, possibly out of doors.'

'That fits quite neatly with what we suspect about his death,' Hennessey said. 'He, if it is who we think it is, remained with one other young man in student accommodation after their mates had gone home at the end of their final year.'

'I see.' Dr Dunn laid the cocoon in a glass dish. 'Doubtless you'll be wanting to have a chat with the other man?'

'Doubtless we will.'

'Well, I can tell you he died a violent death.'

'Oh?'

'Yes. Turning to the mouth once again, I note a distinct red hue about the teeth – faint, but it's there. It's caused by the bursting of blood vessels that occurs during bouts of violence. He could, for example, have been strangled and put up a struggle. Other indications of a violent death, bruising, pitochia—'

'Pitochia?' Hennessey asked.

'Small red spots in the inside of the eyelid. They often occur as a result of violence, and other causes, it must be said. But such indications disappeared a long time ago as his flesh decomposed. It would have rotted from within by primary invaders. Second 'The absence of more cocoons laid by flies, the secondary invaders, indicates that he was buried quickly after his death. Probably not placed in a prepared grave, because at least one fly had time to find him, but one dug immediately afterwards. The grave seemed to me to be about two feet deep, in good stone-free soil. A strong man could have dug the hole in a few hours, within the space of a summer's night. He would have made a bit of a noise, but he would have had to take that risk, and that's really your territory. Then he would have been covered over very quickly. That might, just might, indicate premeditation. But again, that's your territory.'

'Even so, why do you say that, Dr Dunn?' Shetland asked.

'Well, there didn't seem to be a layer of soil between the concrete and the bones. You see, the absence of

175

signs of large-scale primary-invader activity means he was covered over immediately he was put in the grave. Had his murder been unpremeditated, then I would have expected the murderer to dig the grave, put him in and then cover the body with a layer of soil, to give him some time to go and buy some cement. But in the event it appears that cement was poured directly on to the body, indicating that the cement had already been acquired prior to the murder. I can't see students, or recent graduates, doing building work on property they are renting. But your province, not mine.'

'None the less it's a valid observation. Thank you.'

'I think I have come to the end of this p.-m.' Then, for the benefit of the tape recorder, he said, 'The cause of death is not determined, but indications given by the red hue in the teeth indicate that this person met a violent end. I'll take a cross-section of one of his teeth and work out his age. I'll be able to let you have that information tomorrow forenoon at the earliest. But he was a short, finely made young man when he died.'

'Thank you.' Shetland smiled his thanks, as did Hennessey. 'That's plenty for us to be going on with.'

Walking out of the imposing Gothic nineteenth-century part of St James's to the car, Shetland glanced at his watch. 'Four thirty, close enough to the end of the working day for me.'

'And me,' said Hennessey. 'I put in more overtime than I get early finishes. I can square a four-thirty finish with my conscience.'

'You'll be travelling back to York?'

'Yes.' Hennessey found that he and Shetland fell easily into step with each other and occasionally nudged shoulders.

'Anybody at home?'

'Just a mongrel.'

'Oh, I'm sorry.'

'No matter.' And Hennessey told Shetland about his glowing memory of Jennifer, and of the significant other in his life. 'But we have decided not to merge households, not at our age. Do you have a family?'

'One wife of many years, two children making their own way. You travelling back to York by train?'

'Yes, via Harrogate. Slower than the Crossgates route but infinitely preferable, a lovely scenic line.'

'I know it. That view of the river at Knaresborough. So how about a beer before you travel? There's a quiet bar in the Queen's Hotel, about the only place in Leeds city centre where you can have a beer and a conversation without having to raise your voice.'

'Love to.' Hennessey turned and made eye contact with Shetland. 'Love to.'

Eight

In which George Hennessey meets a chartered accountant for lunch and learns of an unsolved crime

MONDAY 11 APRIL

It was the one compensation Hennessey had found that always obtained to very old murders: the pace of the investigation was pleasingly leisurely. He had passed a quiet weekend, on duty on Saturday, when little of consequence for the CID took place. He had received a fax from Tom 'Pony' Shetland relaying information from Dr Dunn of St James's to the effect that a cross-section of the tooth taken from the skeleton found in the rear garden of 278 Brudenell Road had enabled Dr Dunn to determine age at death to be twenty-two years, plus or minus twelve months. Underneath the typed officialese, a neat hand, evidently that of Tom Shetland, had written, 'You owe me a pint.' Hennessey smiled, replied with a handwritten thanks and added 'next time you're in the famous and Fayre'. Sunday he had spent quietly at home, continuing with the account of the Peninsular War, taking Oscar for an extra long weekend walk as was their custom, and lamenting that he could not have had some time with Louise, but she and Samson and her two daughters were attending horse trials at Bramhope.

178

And so, after a succulent leg-of-lamb roast for his evening meal, he strolled into Easingwold for a pint of stout at the Dove Inn and strolled home again, enjoying the walk more than the beer (though the beer was by no means an ordeal for him).

The following morning, each holding a mug of steaming coffee, he and Yellich sat in his office. Hennessey told Yellich of the findings of the post-mortem that had been conducted the previous Friday at St James's Hospital. Then he said, 'So what have we got?'

'Got?' Yellich shook his head. 'An awful lot of smoke, plenty of that, but actual evidence that links anybody to anything, precious little. What we have is very old. No warm corpses and identifiable figures seen running away, not on this one. The most valuable twenty-four hours after any murder is long gone.'

'Had the same thought myself over the weekend, Yellich.' Hennessey stirred his coffee with a ballpoint pen. Hennessey didn't take sugar and the action seemed to Yellich to be the gesture of a man lost, but wanting to do something. He understood, and felt for his senior officer.

'There's a way in, boss,' he offered encouragingly. 'There has to be.'

Hennessey looked at him. 'That's three bodies so far. Well, one whole body, bits of two others, and all connected to a man who calls himself Quinlan but who fits the description of one Clement Drover, once known to his adoptive mother as "the Cuckoo". He got comfortable in their nest and sucked it dry.'

'Time for a quiz session with him, boss? Pull him in for questioning? Make him sweat a bit?'

'Oh, he's sweating all right. Did you see the regional news over the weekend?'

'The report of the skeleton we found at the rear of the house in Leeds? Yes, I did, boss.'

'And so will he have. He'll have worked out that we followed the trail from the skull of Amanda Dunney to the skeleton in the back garden – or maybe he won't. Two separate police forces: he may assume that the two discoveries are coincidental, and he'll also know there is little, evidentially speaking, to link them with him. Besides which he can't go to ground.'

'Can't he?'

'No. Not if he is passing himself off as Andrew Quinlan Esquire, chartered accountant. Hardly a member of the criminal fraternity, with bolt-holes and hard cash and false passports stashed away. No, I think he'll try to keep calm and cool and continue to act quite normally. He's clever enough to know that if he does do a runner he's only flagging up his guilt, because only the guilty run.'

'Good point, boss.' Yellich sipped his coffee. 'So what's for action?'

'Deoxyribonucleic acid.' Hennessey smiled. 'Are you impressed? Took me a long time to learn how to pronounce it.'

'DNA to oiks like me.'

'And oiks like me too, Yellich, but yes, DNA. Can you contact the forensic science laboratory at Wetherby?'

'Yes, boss.'

'They'll have to liaise with Dr D'Acre here at York and with . . .' he consulted the fax that he had received on Saturday, 'with Dr Dunn, forensic pathologist at St James's Hospital in Leeds. If they could obtain DNA samples from the headless skeleton examined by our own Dr D'Acre, and a sample from the skeleton which was examined by Dr Dunn and compare them. If they match, and I suspect they will, they'll prove the skeletons to be brother and sister.'

Yellich glanced questioningly at Hennessey. 'But how do we get a positive ID on the headless skeleton?'

Hennessey explained. 'Marian Cox, née Quinlan, travelled to this neck of the woods to find her estranged brother Andrew. She contacted her husband in Salop indicating that she had found her brother. Shortly afterwards she disappeared. At about the same time the loathsome Amanda Dunney also disappeared. Their disappearances, as we have said, have to be connected because bits of the two women may have been found in the same hole. I say "*may* have been found", because Amanda Dunney's skull is still the only positive piece of evidence we have. But if we can use DNA profiling to link the two skeletons as brother and sister, then Mrs Cox, née Quinlan, who was married with children—'

'Ah, a DNA sample from one of her children!'

'Good.' Hennessey jabbed a finger in Yellich's direction. 'The first step is to link the two skeletons. If they don't match, we've gone up a blind alley, but if they do match, we can ask a living descendant of either whose identity we are certain of.'

'To wit, one of Mrs Cox's children.'

'The very same. And if *that* strand of DNA matches, then we have the skeletal remains of Andrew Quinlan, who was murdered about thirty years ago, and the skeletal remains of his sister Marian, who was reported missing about twelve years ago.'

'I can tee that up, boss, no problem.'

'Good. Leave it to you. Me, I'm going to have a chat with the senior partner of the chartered accountant who is calling himself Andrew Quinlan – see what he thinks about him, help me get the measure of the man. Don't want to go to their premises, though, that'll put our man too much on his guard.'

'Invite him for a pub lunch, boss.'

'Yes . . . I was thinking of inviting him to the station, but a pub lunch, yes, that sounds just the ticket.'

'Couldn't resist it.' Bernard Vernon was a tall, broad, man, close to retirement but clearly enjoying good health. He had the smooth skin and the sparkle of life in his eyes that would be the envy of many a thirty-year-old. He served as a good example of the observation that age is a concept, and people age at different rates. 'Can I get you a drink?'

'I'll buy these.' Hennessey asked for a pint of Black Sheep best. Vernon said he'd have the same.

'Shall we order now? I can recommend the chilli.'

'Yes, two chillis, please.' Hennessey placed the order with the white-shirted barman. 'We'll be sitting . . .'

'In the corner?' Vernon suggested. 'It'll be quiet over there.'

'Very good. In the corner, please.'

Vernon and Hennessey carried their beer to the table in the corner of the room and sat under low beams, adjacent to a log fire, amid prints of hunting scenes from bygone times.

'I often entertain clients here,' Vernon explained. 'That's how I know it. Not the big clients; the really big names we take to the Crown Hotel for lunch.'

'I see.'

'So, explain the summons for a pub lunch by a police officer I have not met, and with not even a parking ticket on my conscience. A summons I couldn't resist.'

'Yes . . . I didn't want to call at your offices and I also asked you not to tell anyone whom you were meeting, because I want to keep this as low-key and discreet as possible.'

'Cloak and dagger! The like does not happen in Selby.'

'Well, it's probably in respect of incidents in York and Leeds; many, many years ago at that.' Hennessey paused. 'I want to ask you questions about Andrew Quinlan.'

'Quinlan.' Vernon groaned. The name clearly had uncomfortable implications for him. 'Oafish, boorish . . . treats the secretaries like dirt, and the juniors too. And he's not a particularly good accountant. He's cost us business: clients have taken their work elsewhere because of Quinlan's performance.'

'He's been with your firm a long time?'

'Thirty years. My father is *the* Vernon in the company's title. He started the firm with his mate "Big" Tom Scott over seventy years ago now, just the two of them in a room above a grocer's shop. Now we are one of the largest firms in this part of Yorkshire. It was my father and Tom who interviewed Quinlan. I'm ten years older than he is and I well remember him coming to join us. He proved to be a disappointment almost from the beginning.'

'Really?'

'He came with a glowing reference from his university, a first-class honours degree. But it was his background that intrigued my father and Tom. He'd grown up in children's homes, coming from that disinterested, unstable background to take a first from one of England's most prestigious universities. Well, Dad and Tom thought that took courage; they told me at the time that Quinlan must have broken down the sort of barriers that most people can't even imagine. So he came for an interview, interviewed well and was offered a job. He's been with us ever since. He's grown as we have grown, but more in the manner of a leech, rather than someone who has pulled his weight and made a contribution to the company. And his attitude: not the modest, unassuming, cap-in-hand manner you'd expect from one of his background, but an arrogance of the sort that gives public schools a bad name.'

'I see. What's his appearance like?'

'His appearance?' Vernon seemed surprised at the question, but answered it. 'He's a tall man, distinguished, dresses well, conservatively as we would want, and appropriate for a man of his age and occupation. Still has a good head of hair – light, sandy-coloured . . . Drives a Mercedes Benz now, after many years of being a BMW man . . . Lives in York – well, near York. Other side of York from here.'

'Do you have his address?'

'I could get it for you.'

'I'd appreciate it.'

Vernon dipped into his jacket pocket and retrieved a small mobile phone, tapped two buttons and then held it to his ear. 'Nice thing about being sixty-three years of age is that you don't have to worry about the long-term effects of these "brain fryers", but I don't like to see my grandchildren using them.'

'Wouldn't have one.' Hennessey sipped his beer. 'Don't like the idea of being at people's beck and call.'

'You can switch them off, keep them switched off until you – oh, Penelope, yes, it's Bernard here. Is Andrew Quinlan near you at the moment? No? Good. Can you put his address up on the screen and read it out to me? Thanks.'

He made a writing motion, and Hennessey handed him his notepad and ballpoint. Vernon listened and wrote on the pad at the same time. 'Thanks, Penelope.' He snapped the mobile phone shut and handed the notebook back to Hennessey. On it he had written: *Cuckoo's Nest, East Riding Way, Nether Poppleton, York.*

184

'What do you know about his private life?' Hennessey pocketed the notebook.

'Very little. Keeps himself to himself really, fairly bookish sort of bloke, told us he belonged to a reading group – that was some years ago though. He was less bombastic then. The more overbearing he got, it seemed, the less interested in books he became.'

'Married?'

'No . . . He had a fling with Mary Wright, one of our juniors. That's a sad incident in the firm. She died in suspicious circumstances, murdered in fact.'

'Really?'

'Yes, really. In fact Andrew Quinlan was in the frame for that, as I believe the expression to be, but he had an alibi.'

'Anybody done for it?'

'No, nobody was, unsolved case. It'll still be open, still "on your files".'

Mary Wright, Hennessey wrote on his notepad.

'Why? Are you going to investigate?'

'Possibly, very possibly. Tell me, what checks do you make to determine that people are who say they are when they apply for a job?'

Vernon paled. 'Are you saying . . .'

'I'm not saying anything. What checks do you make?'

'Well, heavens . . . When it comes down to it, I don't think we do make thorough checks. The references would have been genuine, he would have to provide his true National Insurance number, that would be accurate.'

'I'm sure it was.'

'You're not telling me that Quinlan isn't Quinlan? You're not saying he's an impostor? Mr Hennessey, I have to insist that you tell me. If our company is being compromised in any way I want to know about

185

it. I insist you tell me. I have helped you. You help me.'

Hennessey paused. 'Very well, but on the strict understanding that you don't breathe a word of it to anyone, and I mean anyone. If word leaks out it could jeopardise the whole operation.'

'You have my word.'

'And you must try to continue to behave towards Quinlan as if this conversation never happened.'

'Again, you have my word.'

'Well, the real Andrew Quinlan was short and dark-haired.'

'Oh . . .'

'He shared a house with three other accountancy students at Leeds. At the end of the course Quinlan and one other student stayed in the house. The other student was described as blond-haired, well built, and had been educated at a public school. Quinlan took a good degree; the blond-haired student failed his exams.'

Vernon sank forwards and put his hand to his forehead. 'Not the body that was discovered in the back yard of a house in Leeds? I read it in the *Post*.'

'Yes, I'm afraid so. No positive ID that it is the body of Andrew Quinlan – yet. We are hoping to match DNA from his nephew, but the height of the skeleton and its age at death fit the description of Andrew Quinlan.'

'The blond-haired bloke murdered Quinlan and attended the job interview passing himself off as Quinlan, is that what you're saying?'

'Possibly.'

'But how would he know Quinlan's National Insurance number?'

'Quinlan had a job, pulling pints in a local pub. If he left one of his pay advices lying around, that's all it would take. Quinlan and this fellow were mates, they'd know a lot about each other.'

'God in heaven . . .'

'What? Have you remembered something, Mr Vernon?'

'Quinlan's seemed agitated over the last few days, but that's not it. It's the phone call from his sister . . . It must be ten years ago now, possibly more, it's coming back now.'

'What do you recall, Mr Vernon?'

'Well, we were standing chatting in the open area of our office – each accountant has his own office accommodation, and there is also an open area where the secretaries and the word processors are. One afternoon a call was answered by one of the clerical staff, who held up the phone and said, 'It's your sister, Mr Quinlan,' to which I said, 'I didn't know you had a sister, Andrew,' to which he replied, 'I didn't know I had one either,' then laughed and came out with some story about it being so long since they had seen each other . . . but it didn't ring true. I never gave it much thought, but his comment about not knowing he had a sister sounded like a slip, something he regretted saying. You'll have heard people say the like.'

'Many times. Please go on.'

'And his attempt to recover the slip seemed a little opaque. Now it seems downright transparent.'

'I think you're right, I think it was a slip. If the man who is calling himself Quinlan is who we think he is, then he has an *adoptive* older sister, but the real Andrew Quinlan probably wouldn't have told him about his natural sister, and her presence must have come as quite a surprise to the bogus Andrew Quinlan.'

'All these years . . . it explains a lot. Explains why he never left us – he wouldn't get a job anywhere with the reference we'd give him – and if he failed his degree, it explains why he wasn't on the ball as much as we would have expected.'

'You never chopped him?'

'Never was actually bad enough *to* chop; always the weakest member of staff, but never quite choppable. He's clung on with his fingernails.'

'Can we return to the phone call? Do you remember what he said?'

'I remember he was nervous. I remember his voice was shaking. He said not to come to the office, which was reasonable, but to come to his house that evening.' Vernon paused. 'Then he asked if she was alone. I didn't hear her reply but he seemed to be relieved by it. Then he said, "How does lasagne sound?" Which I also thought strange because he always says he's no chef.'

'Do you know when that was?'

'When was it, when was it? Well, I distinctly remember that Dorothy Pugh took the call. She retired on the same day that my first grandson was born. I drove from her retirement party to the hospital to meet my grandson, and he's now twelve years old. He was born in the November of that year. That call was made during the summer months: we stood in shirtsleeves in a hot office.'

'So, about twelve years ago?'

'Yes. I'm going to have to go home . . . I can't go back to the office and act normally towards Quinlan.' He took his mobile out of his jacket pocket, phoned 'Penelope', told her he wouldn't be in for the remainder of the day and asked her to cancel his appointments. He snapped the mobile shut and put it back in his pocket. 'Probably won't be in tomorrow either.'

The waiter arrived with two long, thin plates, each of chilli on a bed of brown rice. 'Chilli, gentlemen.'

'Take mine away.' Vernon waved the waiter away.

'Sir?' The young waiter was clearly surprised. 'Take it away?'

'Yes, I can't eat it, I feel . . . I feel unwell.'

'I can't refund your money, sir.'

'That,' Vernon stood, 'that is the least of my worries. Good-day, Mr Hennessey.' He turned and walked out of the pub.

George Hennessey on the other hand thought that it had been a most productive interview, and tucked into his lunch with relish. He found his mind turning to his son, about the age he was when he wanted to be an astronaut, and how then his favourite meal had been 'stupid bird and brown lice', which was boyspeak for 'chicken and brown rice'. It all came flooding back and seemed like it had been yesterday, just the two of them, father and son, eating a meal together. He let his meal settle, drank the remains of his beer, strolled into Selby, admired the abbey – on that day encased in scaffolding – against a clear blue sky, then walked on to the station and took the train to York.

At his desk in Micklegate Bar Police Station Hennessey picked up the phone and pressed a two-figure number.

'Collator.'

'DCI Hennessey.'

'Sir?'

'File on the murder of one Mary Wright, please. My office, a.s.a.p.'

'Do you have a date for the case, sir?'

'No, but it'll be within the last thirty years, and it is local.'

'Very good, sir.'

Hennessey walked to the corner of his office, where stood an electric kettle, a bottle of instant coffee and a can of powdered milk. He made a mug of coffee and glanced out of his window at a group of tourists walking the walls, then returned to his desk carrying the mug of hot liquid. It was still too hot to drink when a cadet tapped on his office door holding a file and said, 'The collator asked me to give you this, sir.'

'Thanks.' Hennessey took hold of the file, laid it on his desk and began to read.

Mary Wright was murdered when she was twenty-seven years of age. The photograph in the dusty file showed her to have been a vivacious-looking redhead with tumbling hair, and a figure that Hennessey thought would be the envy of many a fashion model, with a face that could sell cosmetics and a smile that could sell toothpaste. In the photograph she was leaning on a rock, wearing a very small orange bikini that matched her hair perfectly. The background of the photograph was that of a beach, of sea, of blue sky. He turned the photograph round and on the back he saw a neat, precise, female hand had written, *Me, taken by Andrew, Kos (last day)*. Mary Wright in happy times; and a lot nearer to her actual last day than she could have thought. And Andrew? Andrew Quinlan? Or another, earlier involvement with a lucky man of the same name? Other photographs in the file were less pleasing to the eye and of interest only to a police officer, being of Mary Wright's corpse, by then bereft of even a bikini, utterly naked, lying face-up in a field. Hennessey laid the photographs on one side.

Mary Wright had been strangled. The post-mortem report revealed a partially digested meal (possibly Italian), which in Hennessey's view meant 'certainly Italian'. He was well aware of the reluctance of the medical profession to commit to a certainty, and so a large quantity of pasta and minced beef richly flavoured with tomato and cheese was 'possibly Italian'. So, she had had an Italian meal before she died. She had also consumed a large amount of vino on her last day. The p.m. report also noted an absence of defence wounds. She did not fight for her life and claw the face of her attacker, leaving a lot of lovely blood and skin tissue residue under her fingernails. No comment was made about this, but for Hennessey the inference was inescapable: she had been wined and dined and, when sleeping off the effects of the meal and alcohol, she had been strangled. Hennessey checked the front of the file: the body had been found one Sunday morning. So a meal on Saturday evening, 'Let's go back to my place' and death by strangulation at, say, 1 a.m. body taken out into the country and dumped with no little contempt for the victim and an attitude of you-can't-catch-me arrogance towards the law.

Never yet having met the man, though with growing awareness that such a meeting was inevitable, Hennessey thought the whole thing had 'Quinlan's' pawmarks all over it. And 'Quinlan' had been interviewed, but all too briefly, and also too superficially for Hennessey's liking. He was her lover at the time, that he didn't deny, but he had no motive to kill her; in fact they were just short of that stage where they would have decided to marry and plan a future together: 'We were engaged in everything but name, she was my future,' he was recorded as saying. The interviewing officer had also recorded that he seemed to be in a state of shock, which looked genuine. There was no overt display of emotion, which would have caused suspicion. In a situation like that an Englishman, especially one of 'Quinlan's' background, was expected to keep his upper one stiff, very stiff indeed. 'Andrew Quinlan' gave his whereabouts that night as with an old university mate in Leeds, which alibi was checked by phone, and then confirmed by written statement. And that seemed

191

to be that. There was no apparent motive to explain the murder of the beautiful Mary Wright, nor any other suspect in the case, and the police investigation seemed to have faltered and then fizzled out for lack of momentum. Other crimes were committed, the attention of the police was distracted, their resources stretched, and the file on the murder of Mary Wright began to gather dust.

Hennessey turned back to the beginning of the file, feeling an annoyance with his predecessors and an embarrassment for the British police. Harry Hill, he read, was the 'interested officer' in the case. Hennessey remembered Hill well: a jovial man for a police officer, but whose joviality and false good humour were a smokescreen to conceal the fact that his feet were not touching the pedals of his job. Harry Hill, the back slapper who called everybody except the most senior officers 'my good mate', had retired to Spain shortly after Mary Wright had been murdered. Nothing was going to get in the way of good old Harry's retirement, and if that meant a myopic approach to the murder of a young woman who had everything to live for, then that meant a myopic approach. Or tunnel vision. Or looking for a reason for not looking further, because there was, so far as Hennessey could see, a huge, huge motivation for the murder of Mary Wright, and which pointed to the bogus Andrew Quinlan as being her murderer.

She had discovered his secret.

And it was probably the reason why the bogus Quinlan had never married. His relationship with Mary Wright had taught him that you can't get married and continue to live the lie that Hennessey now believed him to have been living.

'He's a serial killer.' Hennessey spoke the words to himself before he realised he had done so. 'He's a serial killer.' He walked down the corridor to Yellich's office, entered without the usual polite tap on the door frame, sat – nay, Yellich would in later years recall Hennessey virtually collapsing – in the chair in front of Yellich's desk and said, 'He's a serial killer.'

'Sir?'

'Quinlan. Or the man who calls himself Quinlan. Drover. He's a serial killer. Not in the sense of random victims, nor, I suspect, not in the sense of qualifying for a single to Rampton, but in the sense of being a multiple murderer. This guy has gone through life leaving a trail of corpses behind him.'

'Sir, you're not making sense.'

Hennessey paused. He looked at the floor then looked up, held eye contact with a bemused-looking Yellich and said, 'This is what happened. He's damaged in early childhood, learns fear and survival instinct—'

'Drover?'

'Yes. Gets adopted by a family dripping with wealth. Their social conscience is pricking them, so they scratch the itch by adopting a damaged little street turk, rescue him to turn him into one of them.'

'Except that you can't make a silk purse from a sow's ear.'

'Well put.' Hennessey pyramided two fingers in Yellich's direction. 'Good. Anyway, when living with the Drovers he gets spoiled rotten, gets to believe he can have what he wants. By some twisted logic, he feels he's owed it. Anyway, he's thrown out of the adoptive household because he's caught with his fingers in the family business's till, so he has to make his way in the world using his own devices. Sadly for him his devices are not up to much and he bombs his degree. At the time he's living with Quinlan, who is also alone in the world but who hasn't bombed his degree, so Drover pinches it, and the reference that the university wrote for Quinlan, and Quinlan's National Insurance number. In fact he steals Quinlan's life.'

'Victim number one is the real Andrew Quinlan, buried under a lot of cement in the rear of the house in Leeds.'

'Right. Any feedback on the DNA profiles yet?'

'Not yet, boss, too early in the piece still; all keyed up, though. Mrs Cox's son is giving a DNA sample at the medical centre of his university to a police doctor tomorrow, I think. We'll get a result very soon after that.'

'Good. Anyway, all goes well for Drover, now a.k.a. Quinlan. He doesn't measure up to the expectations of a man with a first and struggles as an accountant, but survives and continues to survive.'

'Though doubtless now worried, boss, since the discovery of the bodies made the press.' Yellich leaned forward, an unusual posture for him when talking to Hennessey who, similarly unusually, sat in a reclined posture.

'They haven't been *linked* by the press, though, have they?'

'No, boss.'

'So, he'll be hoping they remain unlinked. One grave in a field outside York, another in a back garden in Leeds. No reason for the press to speculate, and we're keeping mum.'

'Certainly are, boss.'

'So, boyo continues living a lie, pretending to be Andrew Quinlan. Then he has two potentially disastrous happenings. The sister of the real Andrew Q turns up, and at the same time his girlfriend is murdered.'

'He had a lady-friend?'

'About twelve years ago. I had lunch with his employer today. He declined his food and went home feeling sick.'

'As you might expect.'

'Drover was apparently very flustered but recovered quickly and invited Quinlan's sister to come to his house that evening, promising to cook her a meal, which was surprising for his employer because Drover was apparently no dab hand in the kitchen. So Marian Cox, née Quinlan, arrived at the house, "Cuckoo's Nest", self-parody there all right, expecting to meet her long-lost brother. She was a dead woman the moment she set foot in that house. She was the one person who could and would have exposed him. Can't think what he did to her, I only hope it was quick. We haven't met him yet, but as his personality begins to emerge from reports about him, I wouldn't put it past him to have told her what he had done to her brother and explained why he had to do the same thing to her.'

'Oh . . .'

'But I doubt we'll ever find out.'

'So the loathsome Dunney, withholding morphine from her patients, why kill her?'

'He needed her skull, as we suspected. She was a lonely woman who readily agreed to an invitation to dinner with the reading group at Quinlan's house, except the reading group knew him as "Mr Preston". Guy's had more names than . . . than . . . well, whatever, has had a lot of name changes. Anyway, that evening the reading group consisted of Drover, a.k.a. Quinlan, a.k.a. Preston, and Amanda Dunney, who for the first and last time in her life found herself desired by a man. She was murdered before she ate, otherwise she would have grown suspicious about the lack of other people in the group – a plastic bag as soon as she stepped over the threshold, I would guess. So he has two bodies. He takes the body of Mrs Cox, Quinlan's sister, and the skull of Dunney, puts them both in the same hole, perhaps hoping they'll be found, hoping that we will assume the bones to be those of Amanda Dunney.'

'Having matched the teeth with Miss Dunney's dental records.'

'Right. But he did not anticipate the eagle eye of Dr D'Acre, nor did he know the extent of medical knowledge, to wit pubic scarring only present on a woman who had given birth, and you remember the rest . . .'

'Yes, boss.'

'That explains why he evidently disposed of one skull and one skeleton less skull, and did so successfully, yet placed the other skull and the other body in a shallow grave.'

'Beats me why he didn't simply dispose of Marian Cox's body, leave it at that.'

'The appeal of complexity to felons trying to conceal a crime, Yellich, occurs time after time and it only serves to trip them up, hoist by their own petard. In this case he was just pathologically obsessed with concealing his deception. So much so, that he achieved precisely the opposite effect. I've seen it time after time. They have made our job very easy on occasions. Or as you said, "There's nowt so queer as folk".'

'So, his girlfriend?'

'Also murdered at the same time. Heavens, he murders Andrew Quinlan, then for twenty years lives peacefully and quietly, so far as we know.'

'So far as we know,' Yellich echoed, with raised eyebrows.

'Then in a period measured in days, he kills three women. Amanda Dunney and Marian Cox are reported missing within a few days of each other. Two days after Marian Cox is reported missing, Mary Wright's body is found in a field, naked. She's been strangled. Of the three female victims only one could at that time be linked to Drover, a.k.a. Quinlan, and he had an alibi for the time of her murder. He was "over in Leeds, visiting a friend from university days".'

'That's no alibi, we know now. He couldn't visit a friend from university days, not as Andrew Quinlan, anyway.'

'Which is my thinking. We can blow that alibi; twelve years isn't a long time ago. I can remember conversations I had twelve years ago, recall actual dialogue word for word, as you'll be able to. Then he has another period of peace and tranquillity, then an incident of localised flooding, and a shallow grave is unearthed by a fast-flowing stream.'

'And here we sit. Mary Wright must have seen something.'

'Mary Wright's murder was investigated by Harry "Happy" Hill.'

'I remember him, boss.' Yellich ran his fingers over his scalp. 'Not the best role model for a young detective constable.'

'Harry "Loose End" Hill is what I remember.' Hennessey paused. 'I like your notion of Mary Wright seeing something she shouldn't have seen in respect of the murders: it's too coincidental that she discovered his secret at the time Marian Cox presented in his life. A surprise visit, only to discover him chopping up human corpses in the garden of his house?' He shuddered. 'She was dead the instant she saw that. But her p.m. showed she'd eaten an Italian meal with much wine just before she died. That doesn't fit with her chancing upon something; too, too many unanswered questions, Yellich.'

'Shall we pull him for quizzing, pressure him a little, see how he stands up to questioning?'

Hennessey paused. 'No, I don't think so, not yet. You see, speaking as an old and jaded cop, I don't think we'll ever have enough to charge him with the murder of Andrew Quinlan. He could, for example, argue that Quinlan had died of natural causes, or had committed suicide, that he chanced across the body and saw the opportunity to assume Quinlan's ID, thereby awarding himself a door-opening first. So he's guilty of interfering with the Office of the Coroner, and obtaining money by deception. That vital evidential link which would convict him of the murder of Marian Cox and similarly the murder of Amanda Dunney is missing in both cases. After twelve years all trace evidence will have gone. Wherever the missing bones are, they won't be in his garden.'

'Don't know, boss. Might be worth a look.'

'We'll do it anyway when the time comes, as it will, especially since shallow graves seem to be a speciality of his, but my waters tell me otherwise. No, the way into this case, is via the murder of Mary Wright. We're going back into that case, Yellich.'

A stiff one. Very stiff. The man leaned against the billiard table in the basement of his house and gripped the cut-glass tumbler. They can, he said to himself, suspect what they like, it's what they can *prove* that's the worry. He drank the whisky. So now they've found Quinlan's body, it had to happen. If it can be identified as his then that's my cover shot. He turned and sank into a leather armchair. But I own all this, outright, and I've money in the bank. So I get sacked, I can survive. I've enough to see myself out.

He staggered upstairs to the living room. He thought of Quinlan's sister. Why, he thought, why, why, why did she have to turn up? She had had to go. She would have exposed him. But inviting sad Amanda Dunney to the house was a mistake; he told himself that that was a mistake, should have kept it simple. It had been simple enough to burn her body in the garden, incinerate it down to the bare bones, chop the bones up, drop them one by one into the canal. He should have just done the same thing with Quinlan's sister. 'Should have kept it simple.' He spoke aloud as he ran his toes through the pile of the carpet. Mary Wright, pushy Mary, asked one question too many, she could have exposed him. So what's the weak link? Where is the danger? He glanced up at the ceiling, at the glass chandelier. The weakest link, he told himself, the weakest link is in Leeds. If the police start to link me to Quinlan's murder, and Quinlan's sister, they'll look again at Mary Wright's murder; and if they do that, if they put pressure on Harris the odd-job man . . . It was stupid, stupid, stupid to have concocted the alibi. Harris . . . he has to go, another mouth to be silenced. It is, he told himself, the only way.

Nine

In which an alibi is blown

'She would be nearly middle-aged by now. Twenty-seven plus twelve – thirty-nine.' The woman looked frail – white-haired, arms from which flesh hung in folds – but her voice was strong and her mind was sharp. Her recollections would be accurate. 'Mary was our only child, you know. She was everything to us.'

A saucepan clanged as it was dropped on the kitchen floor; the sound echoed through the house.

'She's a clumsy girl.' The woman winced at the sound. 'Clumsy and lazy. She only washes the top surface of the dinner plates, then she stacks them on top of each other, so the clean top surface comes into contact with the dirty undersurface of the plate on top of it. I've told her time without number, but will she listen?'

Hennessey relaxed in the deep armchair with a floral-patterned cover and glanced out of the lead-beaded window as the postman walked up the path to the front door, posted the delivery through the letterbox and retraced his steps to the road.

'That's the first post,' Mrs Wright said. 'It's late because we're the last house in the last street of his round. I wonder, would you be so good . . . ?'

200

Hennessey levered himself out of the armchair and walked to the hallway to retrieve the mail. As he did so, he glanced along to the kitchen and saw the maid perfunctorily wiping a tureen. She didn't seem even to have turned at the sound of the letterbox snapping shut. Two envelopes had been delivered, one from British Gas, the second from a private company. Hennessey returned to the sitting room and handed the envelopes to Mrs Wright. 'Junk mail and your gas bill, I'm afraid.'

'Junk mail is good mail. Don't sneer at it, Mr Hennessey.' She took the envelopes from him and opened the envelope from the private company. 'You see, if it wasn't for junk mail, your first-class stamp would cost four times what it costs you now, and junk mail keeps the postmen in work. I'm not bothered what they are selling but I do want . . .' She sifted through the papers that the envelope had contained. 'Ah, here it is, business reply envelope, so no stamp necessary.' She licked the envelope and sealed it. 'Now do me a favour.' She handed the reply envelope to Hennessey. 'Post that for me, will you? Because the company who sent me this unsolicited junk has to pay for those reply envelopes, and that further keeps down the cost of your first-class stamp, and all other postage.'

'I'll remember that.' Hennessey slipped the envelope into his jacket pocket.

'I have a nephew who works for the Royal Mail. He told me that.'

'So, Mary?'

'I'm relieved that the police are looking into the case again. I feel we were ill served at the time. What was that man's name? . . . Hill, a policeman called Hill. He'd a superficial attitude to his job, so both my husband and I felt. The whole thing came to a full stop and he didn't seem to look for ways to push it forward. There was no motive to murder her, and her boyfriend was in Leeds at the time, so Mr Hill called it a day. A random attack, he said. "We'll have to wait for the killer to surface."'

'He said that?'

'He said that. And that was his day's work. You see, that's the problem with having only one police force: you can't take your business elsewhere.'

'You could have complained.'

'To what end? Our daughter had been taken from us. We felt defeated. I still do. My husband didn't last long after Mary's death, less than a year. Life just left him. He was sitting in the chair you're sitting in – I hope you're not superstitious?'

'No.' Hennessey smiled.

'Many people have sat there since and have seemed not to come to grief. It was one evening. I thought he was falling asleep. I said, "Come on, Henry, if you're tired, we'll go to bed." I touched him but he was clammy . . . I said, "Oh, Henry, I'm so sorry." He was only fifty-seven. We were the same age, my husband and I. The same vintage.'

'Tell me about Mary's boyfriend.'

'Why? Is he under suspicion?'

'Not really.' Hennessey didn't want to lead Mrs Wright. 'I'm trying to get a picture of her lifestyle.'

'I see. He was a man called Quinlan. Andrew Quinlan. He was a chartered accountant; she was a certified accountant, a lower status than chartered. I didn't care for him. I don't think Henry did either. Nothing we could put our finger on, we both felt that he just wasn't for Mary. There was something insincere about him, too confident . . . he had a look in his eyes that I didn't care for.'

'A look?'

'The eyes are the windows of the soul, chief inspector. His soul was cold, ruthless. There was a coldness in his eyes despite the generosity of his speech. I think that's what I meant by insincere. He talked in a free and friendly way, he showered Mary with gifts, but his eyes were not the eyes of a generous man. I think he had a short fuse, I think he could turn nasty in an instant. I never saw anything like that myself, it's just a feeling I had: a man with a very low threshold of tolerance. He and Mary weren't together for very long before she was murdered so it never developed into anything serious, but I did worry. She was twenty-seven years old, she wanted marriage and a family and I thought, Oh yes, Mary, but not with Andrew Quinlan.'

'I see.'

'I think Mary sensed it too. She seemed quieter in the week before her death, withdrawn. Preoccupied.'

'Did she say what about?'

'She didn't, but she did say, "If you find something out about someone, they become a different person, don't they?" She didn't say anything else, just that.'

'Did she live at home at the time?'

'No, she had a flat in York. She had a flatmate, Sylvia something.'

'Could you possibly remember her name? It could be very important.'

'Yes, give me a second. Stand . . . something. Standing, Standup, Stand-alone . . . Stand . . . Stanton. That's it, Sylvia Stanton. Doubtless she'll be Sylvia something else by now, and possibly living in Canada.'

'Do you know what she did for a living?'

'Oh, same as Mary. She was also an accountant.'

'Employed by? Do you know?'

'A building society rather than a firm of accountants.

Now which one? . . . A small one, not one of the big ones. Had a name which sounded more like a railway company from the nineteenth century.'

'Harrogate, York and Ripon?'

'That's the one. The Harrogate, York and Ripon Building Society.'

'The Harrogate, York and Rip-off, if you ask me.' Hennessey had found Sylvia Stanton to be very easily traceable: a phone call to the Daveygate branch of the building society and a mention of her name, the line clicked and an efficient-sounding voice said, "Sylvia Stanton speaking." One hour later he was sitting in her office. It was a room without natural light, furnished with modern office furniture, blue swivel chairs in front of her desk, and a large framed photograph of mountain scenery on the wall. Her engagement and wedding ring and photograph of two children on her desk spoke to Hennessey of a woman who had married but who, in the fashion of many modern women, in Hennessey's observation, had refused to give up her maiden name upon marriage. 'The pay's dreadful. I could get nearly double what I'm paid here with one of the big societies.'

'No opportunity to move?'

'Oh, I wish, I wish. The jobs are disappearing in the finance sector, the banks and building societies are closing branches. I'm lucky to have a job at all. The salary's been frozen and the pressure is being piled on. I think it's a way of getting rid of staff, make the job unbearable. I confess I'm tempted but my husband is on a temporary contract and I have these two treasures to think about. So I stay at the saltmine. You must be close to retiring, Mr Hennessey, if you don't mind me saying.'

'I don't, and yes I am.'

'I envy you. Must all be behind you. So, you want to ask me about Mary?'

'She was your flatmate, I understand?'

'Yes. And a good friend. I visit her grave when I can, talk to the headstone . . . I must be mad. And each Christmas I buy a miniature bottle of gin and pour it over the grave. That was her tipple, you see, gin, "Mother's ruin".'

'She drank a lot?'

'Oh, hardly at all. But she drank gin at Christmas time.'

'And wine with a meal?'

'Just a glass. Not more, but that night was an exception.' Sylvia Stanton swept a hand through her dark hair. She wore many rings and bracelets, far too many for Hennessey to find tasteful. Her dress too, a loud yellow, didn't seem to be from a high-street department store, and Hennessey reflected that her financial complaints might be due more to her spending pattern than to her employers' parsimony.

'What do you remember about her murder?'

'The murder? Well, nothing. Of the act itself, all I know was what I read in the *Yorkshire Post*.'

'About Mary, then, at the time of the murder?'

Sylvia Stanton chewed the end of her pen. 'Well, I think she and Quinlan were going through a difficult patch; the euphoria of a new relationship was well past. It was as if she was finding things out about him, things he would rather have kept hidden.'

'Do you know that?'

'I don't, not in the sense of details; but the impression I had was that question marks were popping up all over the place. Mary grew up in Wolverhampton, spent the first ten or eleven years of her life there, then her family moved to York. If you live in York

205

and you want to get out for a day, where would you go?'

'Me, the coast, an hour to Scarborough, or the Dales perhaps.'

'As folk do. In Sheffield, where my husband grew up, well, folk there go into the Derbyshire Peak District for a day.'

'And? I mean, the point being?'

'Well, the point is that she told me she once mentioned to him a day trip to Ironbridge. Wolverhampton folk, you see, tend to take the Upper Severn Valley in Shropshire for their days out and Ironbridge, to visit the bridge, is a popular destination.'

'I see.'

'So Mary mentioned having visited Ironbridge and Quinlan said, "Where's that?" And he is supposed to have spent his early years in Bridgnorth, the next town down the valley from Ironbridge. Even though he left at an early age, he would have known where Ironbridge was. So Mary would have thought. Small things like that, but things which have huge implications.'

'Not who he said he was?' Hennessey inclined his head to one side.

'Not said in so many words, but I think that notion had entered her head and was gnawing away at her. And he wasn't very good at his job, she said. That was a disappointment to her, yet he boasted of his good degree, which is a breach of the rules. You don't ask people what class of degree they've got, nor do you volunteer that information about yourself unless it has some relevance, such as in a job interview, for example. So it was a bit of a surprise when he told her what a good degree he had got, and it was a greater surprise that a man with a good degree should struggle in his job as he clearly was doing. Then there was the age gap. He was a lot older than she was.'

'Did you ever meet him?'

'Once or twice. He came to our flat on occasion. Well built, a "smoothie", but he was an accountant, not many beards and denim jackets amongst accountants; they dress up for work, and dress up to go out in the evening.' She paused. 'He became inconsiderate and I think a little untruthful.'

'Oh?'

'Well, the day she died, it was a weekend, a Friday or Saturday night, I can't recall.'

'A Saturday. Her body was found on Sunday morning.'

'Well, that evening, she was due to go out with Andrew Quinlan and he cancelled at the last minute. I mean, when she was dressed, no time to find something else to do, no time to fix up another date – with a girlfriend I mean. He had to visit a friend in Leeds, he said. Some mate from university days of whom Mary had not previously heard, suddenly popped up out of the blue in a state of crisis. I was going out that night with my boyfriend, who became my husband. We asked if she wanted to come out with us but she declined, she'd feel in the way. So she kicked off her shoes and opened a bottle of wine – not like her, but she was angry and upset, and gave us the impression she was going to demolish it. She'd starved all day in readiness for the meal in the evening, but she microwaved up some pasta.'

'She did?'

'Yes, when we came back there was an empty bottle of wine, and the dirty plate from the pasta meal, one of those ready-to-cook numbers that don't taste anything like

Italian food. And no Mary, so I thought she'd gone with Quinlan.'

'But he was in Leeds.'

'He came back. I saw him.'

'When?'

'That evening.'

'In York?'

'Yes.'

'What time was that?'

'About . . . oh, I don't know, say 10 p.m. We had gone to the cinema, left it looking for an eatery, and saw Quinlan in his car.'

'Definitely?'

'No, not definitely, but a well-built man with light-coloured hair, wearing the same fawn-coloured leather jacket Quinlan always wore, driving the same top-of-the-range BMW Quinlan drove at the time. No eye contact with him, nothing particularly distinctive about his car to set it apart from other top-of-the-range BMW, not enough to count as a positive identity in the eyes of the law I wouldn't have thought, but it is enough for me. It was Quinlan all right, driving in the centre of York.'

'Enough to make us have a closer look at his alibi,' Hennessey growled.

'Really? You think it was Quinlan after all?'

'Can't say. What time did you get back to the flat?'

'About midnight as I recall. I've been over that day so often in my mind that I can still recall details after twelve years.'

'You told the police about seeing Quinlan in York at 10 p.m.?'

'Yes. They were anxious that I make a positive identi-fication and when I told them that it wasn't possible – a fleeting glimpse, at night, driving away from me – well, they didn't pursue it once I made it clear I wasn't prepared to say it was definitely Andrew Quinlan that I saw. The guy, a fairly old policeman, mumbled something about not liking witness identification anyway and wanting something stronger. And that was that. Well, then her parents removed her things from the flat, and I left and rented somewhere else. I couldn't stay in there . . . Then it was all over. I just got on with my life thereafter. I think about her a lot though, and each Christmas I visit her grave and pour a measure of gin over it.'

Later that day Hennessey sat in his office. He was wondering if ever in his career he had unravelled not just one, but as in this case four murders, and got so deeply into the case still without having set eyes on the prime suspect. He decided that this case was a personal first for him in that respect when Yellich appeared at the door of his office, tapped on it and entered.

'Thought you'd be interested in this, boss.' He held a sheet of paper in his hand.

'What is it?'

'Fax from Wetherby, boss.'

'Forensic science laboratory?' Hennessey sat forward.

'The very same, boss.'

'Tell me.'

'Well, sir, the DNA tests in respect of Marian Cox, née Quinlan, have been done and the results have been sent to us.'

'That *was* quick.'

'It's as you suspected, sir. Mrs Cox's son's DNA matches that of the DNA taken from the shallow grave.'

'So the skull was that of the loathsome Dunney female, and the body was that of the non-loathsome Marian Cox, who came to these parts searching for her brother?'

'Yes, boss, and the DNA taken from the body in the field, Mrs Cox's remains, matches the DNA taken from the bones buried in the back garden of the house in Leeds.'

'Proving the said bones to be those of Andrew Quinlan.'

'Yes, boss. Brother and sister. Time to bring in that guy, whoever he is, the one that's calling himself Quinlan. Now we know the identity of the human remains in the garden in Leeds, we can arrest him and charge him with obtaining money by deception. He's not Andrew Quinlan, he has no degree at all, let alone a first. Make him sweat, quiz him.'

'And with what do we link him to the murders? It has to be something that will impress the Crown Prosecution Service, whose standards are impossibly high. Remember, it's not for nothing that the canteen culture in this police station refers to the CPS as the Criminals' Protection Service. Take a seat, let's kick it around,' said Hennessey.

Yellich sat, looking a little dejected. 'You know, we haven't even seen this guy Drover yet.'

'I was thinking just that when you arrived just now.' Hennessey paused. 'First he cools the real Andrew Quinlan, but what proof do we have?'

'He was the only other person in the house at the time and he had the motive: he wanted his qualification.'

'So he came back to the house, found Quinlan dead, realised there had been a break-in, surmised that Quinlan had startled an intruder and the phantom intruder had murdered Quinlan. He then saw the opportunity of stealing Quinlan's identity and the future that he could carve for himself with a good degree. So, he buries the body and assumes Quinlan's ID. All he'll cough to is interfering with the Office of the Coroner. Four years max.'

'Marian Cox? Drover was heard to invite her to his

house – I read your recording in the file. And the Dunney woman, only one to get an invitation to dinner at Drover's house. Both disappeared at the same time, both ended up in the same grave, both had links with Drover.'

Hennessey pursed his lips. 'That might, just might, be acceptable, but the concrete coupling, the mechanical link, is still absent. It puts me in mind of that country doctor, married three times, each of his wives disappeared. We know what happened, of course we know, but he was never prosecuted.'

'But we've got bodies, boss. They had no bodies in that case.'

'Good point. The facts weigh heavily against him.'

'And now we have the murder of Mary Wright, who just happened to be Drover's girlfriend at the time of her death.'

'And it appears that she was beginning to find a few things out about him.'

Yellich looked questioningly at Hennessey.

'I've just spoken to her mother and her flatmate. The flatmate particularly spoke of Mary's growing suspicions. She also made an almost positive identification of Drover in York when he was supposed to be in Leeds. Told the police at the time but because it wasn't a one hundred per cent positive sighting they went with his alibi, that he was with a man called . . .' Hennessey consulted the file on Mary Wright's murder, 'Harris, Norman Harris of . . . St Michael's Crescent, number 18, Leeds 6.'

'Leeds 6 again, student-bedsit-land. If that guy Harris was there twelve years ago, he won't be there now.'

'It's worth checking. You see, Yellich, if that alibi was, as I suspect, concocted, it Drover and Harris entered into a conspiracy to mislead the police, and if we can break that alibi, even twelve years later, then we can charge him for the murder of Mary Wright. That will be sufficient to impress the CPS. A broken alibi means guilt.'

'And once inside he might cough to the others?'

'If he has any conscience he will, but I doubt he has. We've never met him, as you pointed out, but I don't think he'll have a conscience. No, I was thinking that a life sentence was still a life sentence, whether for four murders or one; it's still the same porridge. The parole board is unlikely to be lenient when they review his file.'

'Still, I'd like some justice for his other victims.'

'So would I, Yellich, but softly, softly, catchee monkey. Let's pay a call on Harris, see what he can tell us, if he's still at his last known address. If we can break the alibi, *then* we'll huckle Drover.'

'Now, boss?'

Hennessey glanced at his watch. 'Three p.m. Now.'

Harris, Norman, of 18 St Michael's Crescent wasn't at home.

'He's in hospital.' The wide-eyed girl was new in the world, thought Hennessey, straight from home, straight from boarding school, into Leeds 6. That's some impact. 'Blood . . . blood was everywhere. He was lying there . . .' She pointed to the kitchen, further down the narrow corridor. 'I've cleaned some up, but . . .'

'Which hospital?'

'Leeds General. Such a quiet man . . . He's lived in the house a long time, that's his room, ground-floor front; the police have sealed it, as you see.'

'When was he attacked?'

'Last night.'

'Anyone arrested?'

'I don't think so. I found him, thought he was dead, but the ambulance crew found a pulse.'

*　　*　　*

212

'We transfused fifteen pints of blood until he stabilised.'
The doctor was a young woman, softly spoken but very
confident. 'He was a very lucky man. Very lucky.'

'Where was he stabbed?'

'In the chest. Four times. One wound missed his heart
by a fraction of an inch.'

'Can we speak to him?'

'Yes, but don't tire him. He was sedated to help him
cope with the shock, which could have been just as fatal
as the knifing was nearly fatal, so he'll be a little dull.
Shall we say ten minutes? No more.'

'Thanks,' Hennessey smiled. 'Ten minutes will probably be sufficient.'

'Third bed on the left.'

Hennessey and Yellich walked slowly but purposefully
into Nightingale Ward, with beds lining either side of the
rectangular room, and large windows allowing a generous
amount of daylight. It smelled strongly of disinfectant,
and nurses in white coats busied themselves quietly and
efficiently. The third bed on the left was, Hennessey
and Yellich saw, occupied by a gaunt-looking man in
his sixties.

'Mr Harris?'

'Aye.'

'Police.' Hennessey showed Harris his ID. 'Can we ask
you a few questions?'

'Aye.'

Hennessey drew up a chair by the bed, while Yellich
remained standing at its foot.

'You going to nail him?' Harris addressed Hennessey.

'Who?'

'Quinlan.'

'Did he do this to you?'

'Aye.'

213

Hennessey turned to Yellich and smiled.

'Have you made a statement to that effect?'

'Not yet. That's what you're here for, isn't it?'

'Not exactly. We're from York. The Leeds police will be investigating the attack on you.'

'There's no investigating to be done. Quinlan did it. Left me for dead.'

'Why did he attack you?'

'To silence me.'

'To silence you?'

'Aye. I lied for him some years back. Ten years ago – no, more, more than ten years. I told the police he was with me all one evening. He gave me a couple of thousand pounds for the favour.'

'But he wasn't with you?'

'No.' Harris slowly shook his head.

'Do you know why he wanted the alibi?'

'No. He didn't tell me, said it was better if I didn't know.'

'Probably as well for you, really. You may be prosecuted for that, Mr Harris, I have to tell you that.'

'That doesn't matter. So long as you nail him. I keep quiet all these years, then he does this, tries to kill me. He actually apologised. He said, "Sorry, but I can't take the risk," then he plunged the knife into my chest.'

'How do you know him?'

'Odd-jobbing. That's how I make my money. Go from door to door asking if there's any odd jobs to be done. Being doing it a long time, twenty years; got a few regular customers. Met Quinlan that way. He asked me to dig a hole for him in the back garden of his house.'

'Did he say what for?'

'No.'

'Again, that's probably just as well for you.'

'Did a few things for him over the years. He kept in touch when he moved to York, then I didn't see him for years, then he turns up on the doorstep. I was alone, the students were up the pub. He must have been watching the house.'

'Must have been.'

The recording light glowed a soft red. The twin cassettes spun slowly.

'The time is five fifteen p.m., Tuesday, the 12th of April. I am Detective Chief Inspector Hennessey; this interview is being conducted in the premises of Micklegate Bar Police Station in the city of York. I am now going to ask the other people in the room to identify themselves.'

'Detective Sergeant Yellich.'

'Terence Ward, duty solicitor of Rees, Dickens and Mason.'

'Clement Drover.'

'Have to get used to that name again, won't you, Mr Drover?'

Ward cleared his throat and shot a disapproving look towards Hennessey.

'Mr Drover,' Hennessey continued, 'the issue of obtaining money by deception, while serious, especially since you have been doing it for in excess of twenty years, is relatively minor in this case. Now tell us what you know about the murder of Andrew Quinlan.'

'No comment.' He was a well-built man, clean-shaven and expensively dressed, with light-coloured hair and piercing blue eyes, reeking of aftershave.

'And the murder of Marian Cox, Andrew Quinlan's sister?'

'No comment.'

'And the murder of Amanda Dunney? Done to attempt to conceal the identity of Marian Cox's remains.'

'No comment.'

'And the murder of Mary Wright, doubtless silenced because she was suspecting that you were not who you claimed to be?'

'No comment. I was cleared of that murder, anyway. I had an alibi. Can't pin that one on me.' He had a smooth, self-assured manner.

'And the attempted murder of Norman Harris? Yes, Mr Drover, he's alive. The Leeds police are on their way to interview you about that incident. But he told me and my sergeant here that it was you that stabbed him. If your fingerprints are in his room, and if the bloodstained clothing that we found in your house should prove to be stained with his blood, then that is a watertight case against you. Premeditated. Attempted murder. You say "No comment" if you choose to go in the witness In the witness box you have to answer questions, and can begin to help yourself by answering mine.

'No comment.'

'Norman Harris informed us that he lied to the police He told us that there was no truth in the claim that you were with him on the night that Mary Wright was murdered. He lied to the police in exchange for £2,000. A drop in the ocean for you, but a princely sum for the likes of Norman "Odd Job" Harris.'

Drover remained silent.

'Your alibi is blown, Drover. Mary Wright was strangled. No accidental death, no lesser crime of manslaughter there. It's murder. What did you do? Go to her flat when you knew she'd be alone, entice her into your car with endless apologies and an invitation to a nightclub?'

'No comment.'

Hennessey paused, leaned back in his chair. 'It's going to be "No comment" from you throughout this interview, isn't it?'

'No comment.'

Six months later, on a warm October afternoon, Hennessey and Yellich walked out of the sombre buildings of York Crown Court. Hennessey glanced up at Clifton Tower where, centuries earlier, when the tower was made of timber, the Jews of the city had been herded in and burned alive. 'There's a sense of unfairness.'

'Isn't there, boss? But ten years for deception, a life sentence for murder and another life sentence for attempted murder, it's a good result – still the same porridge, as you said once. He'll be in his seventies before he breathes fresh again, boss. If ever.'

'Andrew Quinlan, murdered before his life began, didn't get justice; neither did his sister who wanted only to meet her long-lost brother. And Amanda Dunney, unpleasant woman that she may have been, she still deserved justice.'

'The jury was right not to convict him for those murders, boss. We had no evidence to offer. A partial result is better than no result at all. Let me buy you a beer.'

Hennessey smiled. 'Yes, thank you, Yellich, I'd like that. I'd like that very much indeed.'

At the same time that Hennessey and Yellich walked out of York Crown Court, a man was proving Detective Sergeant Pippa Booth wrong. Having fortified himself with more than his usual amount of whisky, Sydney Lepping, who lived in squalor in Hedon, who never ate on Sundays because the chip shop was shut, who displayed aggression towards the police but who had quickly melted and had keenly accepted the cigarettes offered to him by Pippa Booth, waited until the tide started to ebb and walked into the ice-cold, dark brown waters of the Humber. He forced himself onwards until the water was chest height, until he felt its chill penetrate his body, and then he flung himself forwards and started to swim.

ML.

9/02